Praise for 'The I

'The children have been so
literacy for next term and h;

- *Y5*

'I finished 'The Beltheron Pathway' in the early hours of the
morning – and it was the middle of SATS week!' -
Y6 teacher and literacy co-ordinator.

'I read this book 24/7. I can't wait to read book two!'
– Annabelle, Year 6

'I really enjoyed the vivid descriptions of the beasts and
creatures that Jack encountered.' *– Joseph, Year 6*

'A thrilling style of science fiction, a sidestepping fantasy
into another world you've never seen before.' *– Erin aged 11*

'A spine-chilling, sure-fire hit!' *– Courtenay aged 11*

'This was a fantastic, gripping fantasy which I couldn't
put down. The story was so compelling at the end of every
chapter I was left thinking what happens next?' *– Anna, Year 6*

'I liked how real things were mixed up with fantasy. It made
me feel like I wanted to be in the book.' *– Noah, Year 6*

'Chris Connaughton's fast paced adventure story is a
very enjoyable and compelling read. The plot races from
one dangerous scrape to another. There are some echoes
of Harry Potter and Lord of the Rings, but the world
Connaughton creates is distinct and his own. You can see
the author's reputation as an actor and storyteller in his
handling of speech and conversation.' *– Amazon reviewer.*

'A master storyteller' –
Christopher Day, The Stage and Television Today

REVENGE CAN BE DEADLY!

The
Beltheron
Select

CHRIS CONNAUGHTON

First published in Great Britain in 2009
by
Intext Publishing

A CIP Catalogue of this book is available from
the British Library

ISBN 978-0-9558707-2-9

Typeset in Palatino 10½pt and cover design
by Chandler Book Design,
www.chandlerbookdesign.co.uk

Printed and bound in Great Britain by
MPG Books Group, Bodmin and King's Lynn

To Ekin
Best wishes!

DEDICATION

This is for Mum, who first took me to the library when I
was young, and began that wonderful lifelong journey
into the imagination, literature and stories.
And for my Aunty Pauline, who shared her love of the
cinema and movies, and through them introduced me to
another type of storytelling.

Acknowledgements

The response that I have received about 'The Beltheron Pathway' has helped immensely in the writing of this second book. I would therefore like to say a big thank you to the children, staff and parents of all of the schools that I visit regularly with my plays and storytelling.

In particular I would like to acknowledge the ongoing support and interest in my work that I have received from the following schools:

Sunnyfields School, Kirkby Avenue Primary, Kells Lane Primary, Abbey Juniors, The Priory School, Chaloner Primary, Ludworth Primary, Ringwood Juniors, and finally to the staff and children of Heighington Redmarshal Juniors for including me in an inspiring writer's residential weekend.

THANKS ALSO TO:

Nicky Prentiss and everyone at Biddles MPG for making the whole process so easy.

John Chandler for his striking cover images.

Janet Shaw and Jayne Tuczemskyi for their unswerving support and promotion of my book in their classrooms.

Paul and Nicky Belcher for looking after me so well.

Shelley, Pete B, Carolyn, Becky, Paddy, Pete P, Geof, Simon and everyone at Mad Alice Theatre for the best summer of outdoor Shakespeare (in spite of the rain!).

Emma Richards for spotting errors!

Caroline for absolutely everything else.

...And of course to Alfred Hitchcock.

About the Author

Chris Connaughton trained as an actor and has worked in all sorts of theatres and arts centres up and down the country. He has performed as Hamlet, Romeo and Macbeth, as well as Widow Twanky, the Mad Hatter and Mr Spoon on Button Moon! His television credits include *Byker Grove, The Tide of Life, The Man Who Cried, Tales from the Piano, Call Red, Throwaways* and *Harry.*

In 1997 he set up Intext Performance to write and produce stories and plays for children. He now presents over 120 performances every year in schools throughout the UK. Chris has also performed in France, Germany, Austria, Spain, Italy, Russia, Romania, Japan and South Korea. He has written (and co-written with Paul Harman) more than 15 stories and 6 plays.

In 2009 he directed *Macbeth* for Theatre Hullabaloo.

To order more copies of this book and to find out more about the world of Beltheron go to www.thebeltheronpathway.com

Prologue

It was morning on Atros. The pale sun had been up over the horizon for almost an hour. The early mist which hovered over the lowlands had gone but the chill in the air was still cold enough to reach through to the bones.

If you weren't moving it felt even colder.

And if you weren't moving and you were lying on the ground then it felt so cold that the blood seemed as if it had frozen solid in your veins and you wouldn't be able to get up without crying out in pain as your joints cracked.

The young man hiding in the long grass by the side of the lake knew that if he didn't move soon, then getting up was going to be very painful indeed.

He gently flexed his toes inside his leather boots and slowly rotated his shoulders to ease the stiffness and to get some of the feeling back into his muscles. His eyes however did not move. They remained focused on the same point in the distance, like a kestrel hovering in the sky manages to keep its head and eyes perfectly still and fixed on the ground below.

The young man had been staring at that same place for the last two hours. It was the point where a small clump of trees thinned out on a low hill, and where a narrow road wound across the land towards him.

'If they are coming today,' he thought to himself, 'this is the route that they will take.'

And if they came, he would be waiting for them.

His grip tightened on the handle of his long, silver sword.

The man's name was Tarawen. He was waiting for the rish, the servants of Gretton Tur the Wild Lord. Tarawen had led a band of rebels on Atros now for over five years. Since the defeat of Gretton Tur, and the collapse of his castle two years before, these rebels had continued to pursue the rish whenever they could.

However, for over eighteen months there had been peace and harmony and Tarawen had become almost like a policeman on Atros; a keeper and protector of this long awaited peace. Even so, Tarawen knew that the rebel gangs still had to keep a close watch on the remaining small bands of rish. There were groups of them who still occasionally scoured the hills and woodlands for food or prisoners.

Therefore Tarawen still kept in regular contact with Cleve Harrow and Lord Ungolin, who were his masters on the land of Beltheron. He kept them informed of any strange activity whenever he might notice it.

Tarawen did all this because the rish were his sworn enemy. They had taken from him all that he had ever loved and held dear. He thought every day about those that he had lost. He hoarded his memories of them. He worried in case the passage of time started to rob him of these memories by making them fade. He didn't want his revenge to be dulled in any way.

As he waited, Tarawen closed his eyes to summon up the images again. Closing his eyes made it easier to remember. Thinking very hard about his mother, father, and his two sisters made them spring more vividly into his imagination. Tarawen's mind started to drift away to a time several years before…

...It had been a beautiful morning. He had been allowed to go with his father, Goloren, to the market in Atros City for the first time. Usually he was expected to stay at home with his mother and younger sister, Farron, while his older sister, Petron, travelled with his father to help with the purchases that they needed. Petron and his father always came home from these trips with stories of the exciting sights of the city and the people that they had met. They sounded like strange people to young Tarawen's ears. Many of them were twice as tall as a man, Petron said, some of them with scaly skins, or tiny figures with sharp features and fur on their faces.

She told him tales of the beggars who dwelt outside, under the eaves of the buildings around the market square, and of their ways of pleading with the merchants for a drink of fresh cold water or a few spare copper coins. But there were also men and women of great wealth who frequented Atros City, beautiful people who moved elegantly, dressed in rich, brightly coloured fabrics.

These descriptions had long fascinated Tarawen and he wished that he was allowed to go with his father to see the sights for himself. His other sister, Farron, bored him. She was two years younger than he was and she always wanted him to join in her silly games with her dolls. He was almost ten years old now and he knew that soon, very soon, the day would come when he was given more responsibility. Then he could help Goloren with more important tasks around the home.

Today's visit to the market was the first step towards that new responsibility, Tarawen thought. His chest filled with pride as he walked alongside his father. Together they drew closer to the bustling market square. The other traders and merchants scurried around, calling greetings to each other or arguing over prices.

The whole morning passed in a blur for the young Tarawen. He followed his father to a number of stalls; listened as he haggled with other men over the sale of grain; laughed along as his father joked over a beer with his friends in a brightly coloured tent; felt pride swelling up again as he saw the obvious respect and liking for his father in the eyes of everyone there.

It had been a successful day of trading for Goloren and they returned home with pockets heavy with silver and brass coins.

They were over half way there, walking along a dusty track that led up the side of a hill, when his father stopped suddenly. He was staring at some markings on the ground about ten paces ahead. Goloren moved forwards swiftly and dropped down on all fours to take a closer look. Tarawen followed his gaze. The markings looked a bit like hoof prints, he thought.

Tarawen stepped up behind his father and looked down at the large prints in the ground. They were like horse's hooves, but pointed at the front rather than curving round. There was another, smaller hole in the dust just behind each print that looked as though it might have been made by a sharp spike or claw. His father stood up next to him.

'Holva prints,' Goloren said in a low voice. 'Rish steeds.'

Tarawen looked up at his father and saw that his jaw had set into a firm, angry line.

'Come, my son, we must get home. Quick as you can now!'

Goloren was already running on ahead. Tarawen hoisted his pack into a more comfortable position on his shoulder and hurried after him.

Before they had gone much further he saw black smoke drifting up on the horizon. It swept up over the brow of the rising hill that led to his home. For a moment his father stopped in his tracks and stared. Then he ran on again, reaching for something in his belt as he did so. Tarawen saw something bright flash in Goloren's hand. Then he was left behind as his father's urgency carried him away and up to the brow of the hill.

When he got to the top, Goloren stared down the other side for a brief moment, down towards their home. Then he spun around and waved with his hand to Tarawen who was still struggling up the hill behind him, warning him to get down. The look in his father's eyes was enough to frighten Tarawen into obeying instantly.

He dropped down into a clump of tall grasses at the side of the path and peered out. His father had turned back to look over the hill again, but his left hand was still stretched out behind him, the fingers splayed, gesturing to Tarawen to stay where he was. In his father's right hand, Tarawen saw the bright flash again, and this time he could tell that it was a dagger.

Then they heard the scream.

With an anguished cry, Tarawen's father plunged down the other side of the hill and out of sight.

Tarawen squirmed in fear and frustration. It was maddening not to know what was going on just beyond his reach. His father had told him to stay where he was, but surely it wouldn't hurt just to take one peek? There was so much noise and uproar on the other side of the rise now that nobody would notice if he just stuck his head out a little way, would they?

Moving as slowly and silently as he could manage, young Tarawen edged his way over the grass. He moved flat on his belly, using his elbows to push himself through the tall stems.

At last he reached the brow of the hill. Cautiously he peeped over the edge and down into the valley below.

The sight that met his eyes filled him with horror and outrage. His home was ablaze and dark smoke billowed from the thatched roof of the farmhouse. Flames flickered through most of the shattered windows. He looked around avidly for any sign of his mother or sisters, but they were nowhere to be seen. There were seven or eight rish galloping around on their terrible holva creatures. The rish themselves had four long arms each, and grey, egg-like heads with small slits for eyes. Their holva were like horses, but with dark skulls and blazing fiery eyes. They had grey scaly skin like a lizard all over their bodies instead of horse hair.

The fences of the corral had been broken in several places and his father's own horses were running wild. They neighed in fright as the holva galloped madly among them, snapping with their jaws. Even at this distance, Tarawen could see the terrified rolling of the horse's eyes.

Goloren was already in the fray of fighting and Tarawen felt a quick surge of excitement as he saw his father's dagger flash quickly among the rish, bringing one of them to the ground. It was immediately clear though that his father could not defeat so many. As Tarawen watched helplessly, one of the largest rish pulled back his bow with his strong upper arms and sent a bolt flying towards Goloren's heart. Tarawen cried out a warning in anguish, but it was too late. The shaft struck his father squarely between the shoulders. He staggered, and Tarawen heard him gasp with a strange, surprised sound.

His father tumbled to the ground. A second rish, on a dark grey holva, cantered casually towards him as he struggled to get to his feet. The rish raised his curved scimitar above his head and began to swing it down in a wide arc towards Goloren's neck. Tarawen gasped and spun around, covering his face with his hands so that he would not see.

He remained there, sobbing for long minutes until the fearful battle sounds receded and all that reached his ears was the crackling and popping of the fire that still blazed in the farmhouse.

Tarawen wiped his eyes and took his hands away from his face. He took several deep breaths and stood up. His legs trembled for a few moments, but he steadied himself and turned to walk down the hill towards the remains of his home…

…Tarawen blinked a tear from his eye at the memories. He remembered finding his mother and sisters at the back of the house. He remembered covering his father's body with his own cloak and burying all of them side by side with a simple white stone to mark their graves. He remembered the tears he had shed and the feelings in his heart.

On that day he had sworn eternal revenge on the rish and whoever they worked for. He shifted his position again slightly and rotated his shoulders once more. They were stiffening up again.

The sun was now high in the sky. It could take hours yet, or days even, before the rish came. He knew that, but he didn't mind the waiting. It was all part of his revenge for what had happened to his family. That revenge would never end until Tarawen himself drew his last breath. He adjusted his position slightly and tightened his grip on the hilt of his sword.

He settled back into the long grass and continued to wait.

Going Home

It looked just like an ordinary street. In fact, most of the time it *was* just an ordinary street. There was the same number of cars parked in front of the houses up and down on both sides as on most other city streets. There were the same front doors and letterboxes and the same arrangements of curtains and blinds that you might see on any street anywhere in the country. At number 23 the blinds were drawn even though it was the middle of a bright spring morning. The trees in the garden were just beginning to show the first green buds.

But on this particular day, this street was anything but ordinary.

Suddenly, behind one of these trees at number 23, hidden from view to anyone who might have been walking or driving by, there was a soft shimmer in the air. A low humming, droning throb began. It was quickly followed by a bright flash of light. A boy appeared where a moment before there had been nothing. The boy immediately jumped behind a bush in the corner by the wall, pushing himself down to the ground where he could not be seen from either the street or inside the house.

He was about 14 years old and wore jeans and a dull green sweatshirt. There was a small rucksack on his shoulder and he carried a glass vial containing a thick liquid in his hand. The most immediate thing you noticed about him though was his hair. Originally dark there were now several streaks of pure white running through it. He was growing his hair long; it was already down to his shoulders and swayed as he moved.

Swinging the rucksack off his back he hurriedly hid the vial away in a secure, zipped pocket. After gazing at the windows of number 23 for a few moments he got to his feet. The boy shook his head and staggered a little, as if he was dizzy; as if the strange, sudden appearance out of thin air was something he was still not used to. (In fact, he had intended to arrive inside the house itself, but his concentration had wavered in the last moments and thrown him slightly off course.)

With three strides he was across the small garden and up the steps to the front door.

Looking quickly behind him to check that the street was still empty he dug a small silver key out of his jeans pocket. He weighed it in his hand as if wondering whether to try it or not. After a moment's hesitation he put it into the lock and tried to turn it.

Nothing happened.

He grinned, but there was no humour in his expression. It was a sour, fixed smile.

'You *did* change the locks,' he said to himself under his breath. 'Huh! I knew you would.'

He gestured with his hand towards the door handle. There was a slight click from inside the door and the handle turned smoothly. The boy moved his open palm towards the door and it swung open. He stood motionless on the threshold for a brief moment before stepping in. He closed the door behind him silently.

It was quite dark in the hallway, with just a few slants of sunlight coming through a gap in the blind that covered the small window next to the door. The boy knew the layout of the rooms though, even in the darkness. He knew it perfectly. He should do, for this was the house where he had grown up.

The boy stood quietly, his head cocked slightly to one side as he listened for any movement within the building.

Satisfied that he was alone he unzipped another pocket and brought out a small glass globe about the size of an apple. He whispered 'illumen' to the globe and it began to glow with a bright orange light. The light spread until it filled the hallway and staircase in front of him.

Everything looked so familiar as he looked around. It seemed as if the lock on the front door was the only thing that had been changed. The same plain, pale carpet, the same ornaments on the side table half way down the hall, the same heavy wooden doors leading off to the dining and sitting rooms and to the kitchen at the end. Everything suggested to visitors that this was just an ordinary house belonging to an ordinary family.

Yes, everything here seemed exactly the same but, since the last time he had stood on this spot, his whole life had changed. This was no longer his home. He no longer felt comfort or safety here, just a blankness in his mind and a dull ache in his chest.

When he had lived here his name had been Jack Anders and he was the only child of parents called Peter and Sophie. Now, two years later, he knew that his name was really Serrion, Serrion Melgardes. His real mother's name was Korellia and he had an older sister called Orianna. Everything he had been told as a child, everything he had experienced while he was growing up, had been false; he had been used as part of an immense lie, a huge betrayal by those he had believed to be his mum and dad.

As he thought about it all again, the boy took a deep gasping breath, as if he were about to sob with grief. Then he shook his head briefly and gave a grunt of resignation. There was no time to feel sorry for himself. It had been two years since he had discovered that betrayal; two years in which he had tried his best to come to terms with the reality of who he really was and all the strange things that had happened.

His true family and his genuine life were on the world of Beltheron now. He kept reminding himself of that. He was Serrion Melgardes, and he had played an important part in the destruction of Gretton Tur, the Wild Lord of Atros. Tur was dead, along with his most valued student, the *real* Jack Anders –or Jacques Andresen to give him his proper, Belthronic title. However there were still a number of spies, agents and traitors loyal to the Wild Lord who survived. Peter and Sophie Anders themselves– Piotre and Sophia Andresen in the Belthronic tongue – were still believed to travel between the worlds of Atros and Earth, continuing the Wild Lord's evil stratagems. It was possible that they also created pathways to visit Beltheron as well, although they had not been seen there during the intervening years.

Even though Serrion had helped to bring about the fall of Gretton Tur, there was still much to be done before all the dangers could finally be put to rest. There were dangers for Earth as well as for Beltheron. To try to discover Piotre and Sophia's whereabouts and guess at their next move were the important motives for Serrion's return to Earth, where he had grown up.

In the two years since his discovery of the betrayal, Serrion Melgardes had become a serious young man. He seemed to be sunk in his own thoughts for much of the time. And the things that occupied those thoughts most were hatred and the desire for revenge.

He had learned many new skills during those two

years. Under the guidance of Cleve Harrow he had honed his natural ability to open any locks or knots with a simple wave of his hand. He had become adept with a sword and after many long hours of failed attempts he had at last managed to use Harrow's glass vials of magical liquid to travel the pathways.

Serrion had another natural skill as well. During his first visit to Beltheron and Atros two years ago he had begun to have premonitions of imminent danger. A bright red light would appear in his mind's eye, alerting him to an enemy presence. As he recognised this talent he gradually began to use it to his advantage. In the past his foresight had sometimes enabled Serrion to avert disaster for himself and others around him.

He focused again on the reason he was here and remembered the words of his sister, Orianna. 'I have discovered a great deal in the libraries, but there is only one way to follow Piotre and Sophia. You must go back, Serrion. Back to Earth. Only by going back to their home will we have the chance to discover clues to what they might be doing now.'

He had not argued. He knew how important it was to find and capture Piotre and Sophia. Cleve Harrow had not agreed to let him go at first. He had been reluctant to send Serrion back to Earth, and into potential danger. Eventually both Serrion and Orianna had persuaded him. Which is why Serrion now found himself on Earth, in this house that had once been home.

Serrion continued down the hallway. There was a study towards the back of the house, through a door that led off the large kitchen. This was where his mother and father had kept all the papers and records for their business. While Serrion had been growing up he had believed this business to include things like travelling to conferences, providing information and training for big companies. Now he knew that it had all been a front, a disguise for what his parents were *really* doing. They had spent their time preparing information for Gretton Tur and laying the foundations for a successful attack on Earth.

He reached the kitchen and stepped in. It was much lighter in here as the blinds were up and the sun shone brightly through the window. He placed the glowing globe back into his rucksack.

He noticed that the door to the study was slightly ajar. Serrion stopped. This was unusual. His parents – no, he must *not* think of them as that! – had always been very careful to make sure the door was firmly closed behind them. Whenever they left the house it was securely locked. Was there someone here? There couldn't be. He was *sure* that the house was empty.

Serrion considered the door for a few more moments. He could not hear any movement. Perhaps they had left in a hurry. Maybe that was why the door was open.

There was only one way to find out. Serrion stepped across the kitchen.

He was just passing the sink when his eye caught a flash of sunlight coming through the window. It flared brightly on the shining wine glasses on the shelf to his left, making them glare with a vivid red light.

A red light! His premonition of danger!

Serrion stopped in his tracks. He held his breath, blinking to rid his eyes of the red glow.

Suddenly Serrion heard the sound of the front door opening, and heavy footsteps began running down the hall towards him.

Mother and Daughter

Orianna Melgardes was doing what she did best. There was a large notebook on her knee, a pen in her hand, and several old textbooks and illustrations scattered around her feet. She was sitting cross-legged on the floor, scribbling away furiously in the notebook. Her pure white hair was tied back in a pale blue ribbon to stop it from flopping in front of her face as she read.

Every now and then she paused to thumb through the ancient pages of one of the books, her eyes running hungrily up and down the lines of old wisdom. For several years she had been helping Cleve Harrow and Lord Ungolin to discover more about the history of Beltheron and Atros. In the past there had been times when her help had been invaluable. She had warned of possible threats from Atros, and had been able to piece together the meaning of overheard conversations and artefacts brought back by Ungolin's spies, or from Tarawen and the rebels.

The work she was involved in today however was more of a personal study; this was something that she was doing purely for her own interest and enjoyment. She was putting together a history of the pulver, Lord Ungolin's guards and soldiers who had served so bravely against Gretton Tur in the past.

She had first become interested in the pulver because of a particularly courageous young soldier. His name was

Parenon. She had got to know him properly during the events of just over two years ago when he helped to defeat Gretton Tur's army on Atros. In fact it had been Parenon and Cleve Harrow, working together, who finally killed the Wild Lord himself.

Parenon was tall and handsome, she thought. Even though she didn't usually think much of the brashness and loud behaviour of the soldiers, this particular one seemed different to her. She knew he was courageous and committed to serving Ungolin and Beltheron, but there was a gentler side to him as well.

She grinned to herself as she remembered how this brave warrior, who would face any danger in battle, hurriedly looked away if she caught his glance, as if he were scared of her.

Her smile continued for some minutes as she carried on with her work. To tell the truth, she was no longer concentrating on her books as much as she usually did.

Her mother, Korellia came into the room. She carried steaming mugs of a sweet, hot drink that Orianna loved.

It was a good excuse to stop writing for the day. She began folding up her papers and closing the books.

'Have you heard from Serrion?' Korellia asked. 'Did he say what time he would be back?'

'Later today,' Orianna replied.

She did not say anything else. Both she and her brother tried to keep some of their activities a secret from their mother. They both knew that Korellia would never be able to relax if she knew the full extent of her children's involvement with the work of Ungolin and the Cleve. Orianna also knew how important it was for Serrion to discover what had happened to the two people he had grown up with; the two people that he had believed to be his parents. But if Korellia discovered what he was doing, she might put a stop to it there and then.

'I hope he will not be too much longer. The supper is on the stove and I am making one of his favourites tonight.'

'I'm sure he will be back soon,' Orianna reassured her mother. She sipped her drink and felt the warm comforting feeling of being safe at home.

They began to prepare the table for the evening meal. Korellia fussed around, bringing plates and bowls while the smells from her kitchen grew stronger and more irresistible all the time.

The sun was dipping over the rooftops of the town and it began to get dark in the room. Orianna began to light candles and lamps. Although Beltheron had electricity – not to mention many other kinds of magical fires and lights – lots of people, including Korellia, preferred a more old-fashioned, natural method of lighting and heating the home.

As it got darker outside, the warm glow of the lamps grew steadily. Soon dinner was ready and Korellia began fussing about how long to wait for her son.

'He didn't even say how long he would be?' she asked Orianna for the third time in as many minutes.

'I only know that he was studying with the Cleve, and he might have gone to visit Helen on the way back.'

She felt guilty about not being entirely truthful with her mother. But then, Serrion *was* studying with Cleve Harrow, and he *had* said that, if there was time, he would probably stop off to visit their friend Helen. However she had not told her mother that Cleve Harrow was sending Serrion on a trip back to Earth to try to trace Piotre and Sophia. It was meant to be a swift journey though. Serrion was only supposed to go to his old home to look around and try to discover if anyone still lived there, or if they had left any clues behind them. He should have been back by now.

Her mother's worried face spurred her into action. Orianna stood up and moved towards the door where her cloak was hanging on a peg. She reached into the folds of the cloak and brought out a small silver screen. This type of technology was very advanced on Beltheron and all kinds of mobile digital communication devices were used by many of the people. Orianna didn't use hers much though. She preferred to walk over to a friend's house to talk to them face to face. She knew that she could jump on a floating space car designed in whatever shape and style she liked and whiz across Beltheron at fantastic speeds. She could if she *wanted* to. But in the same way that their house was lit with old fashioned lamps and candles, she preferred the more traditional methods of communication and transport.

However, she did agree that sometimes the advanced, modern technology was extremely useful. Like now for instance. She tapped the front of the silverscreen once and a series of images appeared on it. Rooms, streets and faces. Selecting one she touched the screen again and a room in Helen's home appeared, where she lived with her parents, Jenn and Matt.

'Jenia? Matthias?' she called into the screen for them using their Belthronic names. 'Is anyone there?'

After just a moment the still image of the room on the hand-held console shimmered and was replaced by a real-time picture. Jenn's face appeared.

'Good evening Orianna,' she said, smiling. 'Are you well?'

'I am, thank you,' Orianna replied. 'But I am a little concerned. Is Serrion there with you?'

Jenn's face looked puzzled for a moment. 'I don't think he has been here at all today. Helen left some time ago for Ungolin's palace. She is at her lessons there with the Cleve, but I don't think she was expecting him.'

Now it was Orianna's face that clouded over with worry. She tried not to let it show to Jenn.

'Never mind, Jenia, he is probably still with the Cleve himself. I will speak to him.'

They talked for a couple of moments more before Orianna switched off her screen.

She was about to turn it back on to contact Cleve Harrow himself when Korellia came back into the room. Orianna did not want to have a conversation with Harrow on the screen in front of her mother, so she reached for her cloak.

'We think he is still studying with Helen and the Cleve,' she said, feeling another pang of guilt at not letting her mother know the whole truth. 'I will go to fetch him.'

'Don't dawdle, Korellia replied. 'The meal will spoil if I have to keep it warm for too long.'

'I won't.' Orianna was already out of the door, swinging the cloak around her shoulders and hurrying down the darkening street.

Korellia closed the door behind her daughter. She was not stupid. She knew that they were all keeping something from her. But she also knew that it must be important, and that her children would not deceive her unless it was necessary. They were trying to save her feelings.

She knew all this, but it was still difficult for her to face. She had lost Serrion for eleven years; she had thought that he was dead until his miraculous return two years ago. She still shed a tear when she thought of all the precious moments that she had lost while he had been growing up.

Her grief turned to anger when she thought of those who had taken him from her. Piotre and Sophia Andresen - along with that horrible Birdwoman Larena - had kept him hidden away from her for so long. And they had caused her all this misery just so that they could use Serrion to cover up the disappearance of their own son, Jacques, while he was being brought up on Atros and trained in secrecy by Gretton Tur.

She shivered with anger. She was glad that Jacques had been killed when Tur's castle collapsed in Atros City two years ago. She hoped that Piotre and Sophia had suffered the same anguish at losing their son that she had felt when Serrion had been stolen from her.

There was even another twist to this particular story though; another reason for Korellia to hate Larena and the Andresen family. That reason was that Larena had recently confessed to the murder of Korellia's husband many years ago.

'I wish I could have just five minutes alone with that creature,' Korellia often thought to herself. 'I would make her pay for what she has done to me and my family.'

Shaking her head in grief from the painful memories that refused to let go of her, Korellia went back to finishing her work in the kitchen.

Old Friends and New Enemies

Serrion spun around in the kitchen. There was no time for him to hide. He could not even get the vial out of his rucksack in time to create a pathway to Beltheron and disappear through it. The footsteps had almost reached the kitchen door.

From across the room he flung his hand out towards the door and it slammed closed. Concentrating all his energy onto the handle he twisted his outstretched fingers swiftly. The metal handle began to melt, fusing the door-catch into the frame, making it impossible to turn from the outside.

The figure running towards the door crashed into it. The noise in the small kitchen was terrifying. Serrion reached into his rucksack for the vial but the zip on the pocket had stuck. He couldn't get it open!

He could now hear urgent voices behind the door. It seemed that there were two men on the other side. Serrion jumped as a loud bang from the hallway made the door shake; they were trying to kick it down! He turned and ran into the study, picking up a long carving knife from one of the kitchen work surfaces as he rushed past.

As he entered the study, he heard the doorframe behind him crunching and cracking. In moments his pursuers would be through! Swinging the study door closed behind him he locked it with a quick flick of his hand. Even in his frightened, distracted state he noticed immediately that this room had been ransacked. Papers were strewn around the floor and across all the desktops. A tall filing cabinet had been overturned and the drawers forced open. There was no time to wonder or worry about this though. Serrion was already halfway across the study, racing towards the window. The door handle behind him was rattling and the voices were now raised angrily.

'Stand back!'

'Hurry up then! Smash it!'

Still running, Serrion put the carving knife into the rucksack and then tucked it tightly under his left arm while stretching his right hand in front of him. The window shattered and in the same moment he jumped through it. Fragments of the glass cut at his face and hands, stinging him sharply, but he was out into the garden.

As he landed he rolled over so that his shoulder could absorb some of the shock, and used the forward momentum to propel himself back onto his feet and into a run.

Ahead of him was a high wall at the bottom of the garden. He knew it led out onto an alleyway that was usually only used as an access to the garages of the houses opposite. Most of the people in the street worked during the day so right now the alleyway was likely to be empty. He swung the rucksack back over his shoulder as he ran, so that he could leave both hands free to climb over the wall.

He was only a few metres away from it, and preparing to jump, when a small, pink camellia bush nearby exploded into flames. He glanced back and saw his two pursuers standing at the broken window of the study. One had his arm outstretched and there was a thin, metallic object in his fingers. It flared briefly and Serrion ducked and rolled once more. The shot missed him and blew a large hole in the garden wall. Grunting with extra effort, Serrion dashed towards it, leaping through the gap just as a third blast detonated by his ear, sending more brickwork into the air and stinging his face with flecks of stone and cement.

Serrion turned to his left and hurried down the long alleyway. His eyes looked desperately left and right, trying to find an opening. He knew it could only be a matter of moments before his pursuers were through the window and running down the garden after him.

Up ahead he saw a garage with an up-and-over door that had been left open. He hurled himself towards it, hoping that the owner wasn't inside.

He ran into the garage, risking a quick look behind him as he did. He was relieved to see that his pursuers still hadn't reached the alleyway. They wouldn't have seen him run in here! That might give him a few extra seconds.

Crouching down on the floor of the garage he slung his rucksack off his back and reached inside for the knife. He ripped at the fabric of the pocket with it until he could get at the vial of liquid. As his fingers reached into the pocket he groaned with dismay. His hand came out sticky and wet; the vial had smashed! The liquid that would allow him to create a pathway had soaked into the fabric of the rucksack. He couldn't use it to escape!

Getting up he silently crept to the open garage door and peered out. He expected that it was now too late to run off through the alleyway without being seen.

It was just as he had feared. The two men chasing him were now in the alleyway and were looking up and down it. They were both tall and looked burly and strong. They were dressed in black leather jackets over dark coloured sweaters and trousers. Every inch of them looked unfriendly and dangerous.

The two men began making their way along the alley,

looking into dustbins and rattling the handles of the other garages, checking to see if any were open. Luckily, as yet, they had not noticed his hiding place. But Serrion knew he only had a minute, at best, before they did.

Serrion shrank back into the shadows of the garage. He looked around to see if there was any other way of escape. There was a door at the other end of the garage. He thought that it must open out into the garden of the people who lived here. He stepped towards the door, holding out his hand to unlock it.

Just as he did so he heard voices from the other side of the door. People were coming down the garden path! Serrion froze. His eyes darted around the garage to see if there was any place to hide. Most garages, he remembered, were filled with all sorts of rubbish, tools and large, empty boxes that might have helped to hide him; ironically, this garage was neat and tidy. With the threatening men behind him in the alleyway and more people on the other side of the garage door there was nowhere to go. He was trapped!

The door suddenly creaked and swung open. Two boys walked through.

'So I told the maths teacher that if he couldn't even add up seven and …' the boys stopped in their tracks and stared at Serrion.

'What are you doing in our - Hey! Jack? Jack Anders? It is isn't it? Blimey! Where have you been hiding yourself all this time? It's been years since…'

The boy who had recognised him spoke in a loud voice. Serrion made desperate shushing signs with his arms, glancing behind him, but it was too late. The sound of running footsteps on the gravel of the alleyway could be heard coming towards them. He had been discovered.

'No time to explain,' hissed Serrion. 'Follow me!'

He raced past the two boys through the garage door

and into the garden.

'Hurry!'

The boys followed him quickly, intrigued at their long lost schoolmate's sudden reappearance and his bizarre behaviour. Serrion threw out his hand and the door slammed and locked behind them, just as the two men raced into the garage.

'Wow!'

'How did you…'

'Who are those men? Are you in trouble?'

'Come on,' Serrion continued. 'We have to get out of here.'

He recognised the two boys now. They were brothers and the oldest had been in the same class as him at school. They had sometimes come to his house to watch DVDs in the evenings. Their names were Adam and Joel, he remembered.

'You *are* in trouble, aren't you?' Adam, the oldest boy, asked again as they ran into their house.

'You could say that,' Serrion replied.

'Are those men the police?'

'I doubt it.'

'Shouldn't we phone 999 then? There's no one else here. Our parents aren't back until tonight,' Joel said.

'No time,' Serrion replied. 'Let's just get out.'

By now they had moved through the house to the front door. Serrion kept looking behind them, checking to make sure that they weren't yet being followed. There was no sign of his pursuers yet. Perhaps the appearance of two other witnesses had made them rethink their plans.

'So where *have* you been?' Joel insisted. 'We were told you'd all moved up to the north, but I know that I've seen your mum and dad at the house from time to time.'

'That's right,' Adam continued. 'They turn up about

every three or four weeks, stay two or three days and then disappear again.'

Serrion's ears pricked up immediately. If they had seen Piotre and Sophia around, then these old friends of his might be able to help him in more ways than one.

'So what *are* you doing anyway?' Joel asked again.

'It's a long story,' Serrion said.

'Excellent!'

'We like stories!'

Adam had started to fumble for his house keys, but when he looked up the door was already wide open and the boy he knew as Jack Anders was halfway down the path to the road.

'That's funny,' Adam thought as he followed Serrion outside. 'I could have sworn I locked that door earlier.'

Serrion's two pursuers decided not to break down the garage door to follow the children. Their master, Piotre Andresen, had told them to be discreet and not to draw any unnecessary attention to themselves. They had been making regular visits to the Andresen house in London. They came to collect the post and papers when Piotre and Sophia were too busy to return to Earth themselves. Until now the two men had succeeded in never being spotted. So instead of chasing the children through a strange house, where there could have been adults incensed and enraged to find two burly intruders, they turned and ran back out of the garage. They sped towards the opposite end of the alleyway where it turned to the right to bring them out onto the road in front of Adam and Joel's house.

The two men were fast, in spite of their bulk. Most of their weight was hard, tightly packed muscle. Both men had trained hard until they could outmatch any boxer in his prime. Their training had given them stamina as well as strength and over a long distance they could catch and outpace all but the fastest of runners.

On top of all this a new urgency now drove these two on. It was essential that they catch this boy who had broken into their Lord's home. The larger of the two, a thug called Karion Bargoth recognised him immediately from his white streaked hair.

'Did you see him, Lathe?' he grunted as they ran. 'That's the Melgardes boy that is!'

'I saw him,' his companion, Lathe Heckle replied. 'And he's faster than I imagined.'

'We'll get him though,' Bargoth continued. It takes more than a skinny whelp like him to get the better of me.'

They had come out into the main road already. Sure enough there was Serrion, breathlessly talking to two other boys. Bargoth and Heckle grinned briefly at each other. The children were less than twenty metres away. They could catch them easily without even breaking into a sweat.

Bargoth took a quick look around him as he began to run towards the boys. They still hadn't seen him or Heckle. There was no one else on the street so Bargoth raised his slim metal rifle to aim directly at Serrion's head. He knew what a prize Serrion would be to Piotre and Sophia Andresen – dead or alive – and he had not a moment's hesitation or pang of conscience about shooting an unarmed boy. He was a trained killer and was just doing his job. In fact, he prided himself on being particularly good at it.

Bargoth now slowed his run to allow himself a better aim. Too many times he had seen others mess things up at this last moment by rushing, or not waiting to take that extra deep breath to calm and steady their muscles from shaking with exertion as they made their shot.

In the same moment that Bargoth readied himself for

the kill however, Serrion suddenly raised his eyes and saw the two men. He began to lift his hand and shout a warning to Adam and Joel as Bargoth pulled the trigger…

Strange Practice

Helen Day was practising her lessons. However, these lessons were very different from the things she had to learn at school. There were no sums to solve, no adjectives to fit into a piece of writing, and no need to remember capital cities or the reasons for the Iraq War.

She was not in a classroom with twenty or thirty other students, but in a room on her own. It was in the middle of Lord Ungolin's palace. Instead of maps and students' work decorating the walls, strange signs and images had been carved into the plaster. There wasn't even a teacher in the room. Helen was all alone facing a glowing, humming, floating sphere the size of a tennis ball. The ball had been motionless in the air for nearly five minutes and in all that time, Helen's gaze had not shifted from it.

She had been silent for the whole of those five minutes, but now she spoke slowly, a single word uttered under her breath.

'Eupheuis.'

Nothing happened at first. Then, after a moment, the sphere began to change shape. She blinked twice, quickly. The ball began to grow in size. It opened out into a flattened egg-like object before sprouting shoots and tendrils like a growing plant. These tendrils extended and then began to feel all around in different directions until one of them reached the wall of the study room. The other shoots immediately turned and sprang towards the wall. The object began to climb down the wall on its tendrils. As each feeler touched the surface a small crack appeared in the plaster and fragments of dust began to fall to the floor.

'Reversium!' Helen called suddenly. The sphere resumed its normal shape, the tendrils shrank back inside it and it fell to the ground. Helen ran to pick it up, gazing at the damage done to the wall as she did so.

'Oops!' she thought. 'That wasn't supposed to happen.'

She had no time to worry about the repercussions of her mistake though. The door opened at that moment and Orianna walked into the room. She smiled a greeting at Helen.

'Orianna! Have you brought Serrion with you?'

Orianna's face clouded. 'No. In fact I came here to find him. I thought he might have returned from the errand that Harrow sent him upon.'

'I haven't seen him all day,' Helen replied. 'He should be back by now.'

She thought for a moment then her eyes lit up. Anyone who knew her would have recognised the flash of mischievousness that lurked there. 'Orianna, do you have anything with you that belongs to Serrion?'

Orianna considered for a moment. She seemed to blush, Helen thought, as if she felt guilty about something and wanted to keep it to herself. After a brief grin, Orianna put her hand up to cover her mouth in embarrassment and then nodded to Helen. She reached into one of the pockets of her robe.

'I do carry this around with me.'

'Something belonging to Serrion?'

'You could say that, I suppose.'

Orianna brought out a small silver locket.

'I know it probably seems foolish and sentimental,'

she said. 'But this is very important to me.'

There was a tiny clasp at the side of the locket. Orianna pressed it with her finger and with a click the locket sprang open. She shook something out of it onto the palm of her hand and gave it to Helen.

'See? It's just silly.'

Helen looked down at her hand. Lying there was a small twist of black and white. With a little gasp, Helen realised immediately what it was: a lock of Serrion's hair.

'Oh, Orianna! It's not silly at all. I think it's beautiful that you should keep this.'

'He doesn't even know that I have it, but it always reminds me of when we first discovered that he really was my brother. This hair was the proof you see.'

The snowy white hair was a feature of Orianna's family. When everyone was in such confusion over Serrion's true identity, his first strands of white hair had been all the evidence that Orianna had needed to know for certain that he was in fact her long-lost brother. There was no surprise that Orianna had wanted it for a keepsake.

'I promise you can have it straight back,' Helen said.

She moved to a table at the corner of the room. On top of it was a well worn dark leather bag. She rummaged around inside it for a moment before lifting out a small vial of liquid.

Orianna guessed her intention straight away. 'Are you sure you should do this, Helen?'

Helen's recklessness made her grin even wider. 'Of course! It's the quickest way to get directly to him. What's more, if he is in danger, then we can bring him straight back here. I just have to take this with us as well.'

She took a small volume from the bookshelf on the wall to her left and tucked it away safely into the leather bag.

Orianna felt herself quite carried away by Helen's enthusiasm. 'What harm can it cause?' she thought to herself. 'Alright,' she said to her young friend. 'But I'm coming with you!'

In another room in Ungolin's palace three people were avidly concentrating on a very different sphere to the one that Helen had been practising with earlier that morning. It was about one and a half metres in diameter and a flickering blue light - like lightning on a dark night - occasionally rippled over the surface. The sphere was supported from the ceiling by strong, thick cords of silver.

The sphere was a most curious sight. But inside it there was something even more strange. Sitting in the centre was a human form. It was a woman, but this one had been shrunk down to the size of a raven. There was enough room inside for this small figure to walk around, but she remained seated and motionless.

Jenn and Matt, Helen's parents, had just arrived and were talking with a large bearded man called Cleve Harrow. They were discussing what to do with this strange creature.

'It's odd, but I almost feel sorry for her,' Jenn was saying.

'Sorry? After everything that she did – and all she tried to do to our family?' Matt replied. His wide mouth was set into a grim line.

'She deserves to stay here in her prison sphere forever,' he continued

'She is fed regularly and her health is monitored,' Cleve Harrow added. 'It may seem cruel, Jenia, but what else can we do with her? If she were released she holds so much anger and hatred towards us all that she would immediately begin causing havoc and destruction.'

Jenn hung her head in resignation, her waves of curling brown hair covering her face.

'I know,' she said in a low, flat tone. 'If she had succeeded two years ago then both Helen and Serrion would have been dead now, and who knows what other terrors she would have helped to unleash.'

'She *must* remain a prisoner in the sphere,' Harrow insisted. 'The power that it contains saps her strength and prevents her from changing her shape again. As long as she remains within it she does not even have the power to break the glass.'

As if in response, Larena slowly got to her feet. Gazing defiantly at the Cleve she walked towards them to the edge of the sphere. As she moved, her glass prison began to sway slightly from side to side on the silver cords. Raising her arms, Larena touched the glowing blue surface. In the instant that her fingers touched it there was a loud crackling noise of static and the blue lightning bolts rippled more violently over the whole globe. Larena's face contorted with a rictus of pain but she did not remove her hands. Her grimace of agony slowly changed and her mouth slid into a fearful grin. Her eyes still held those of the Cleve. He, Jenn and Matt stared in horrified fascination at their enemy, contorted by the crackling blue light that enveloped her.

Larena managed to hold onto the glass for another ten seconds or so before her grin slipped back into a grimace and a shriek of pain burst from her mouth. She sprang back to the centre of her prison sphere. Her shoulders rose and fell rapidly as gasps of breath shuddered through her. She wrapped her arms around herself to hold her trembling form still.

After a few moments she slowly raised her head to look at the three of them. Her small dark tongue shot out in fury and she spat at them. The thick spittle hit the glass which gave another burst of static, blue fire.

The anger, hatred and defiance of the small figure made Jenn tremble. Even with her husband and Harrow standing on both sides of her, and having just seen how secure the prison sphere was, she was terrified by Larena.

'You're right,' she murmured. 'There is no question about it. Who knows what evil that rage could do to us all on Beltheron? We have to keep her in there.'

With a nod from Harrow to the others, all three spread out their hands in front of the globe and it began to shrink. Larena started to get smaller again as well, so that she and the globe remained the same comparative size. Soon she was reduced to the size of a robin and her glass prison was now only the size of a large paperweight. Harrow unhooked it from the chains that were now hanging limply and carried it in both hands out of the chamber and down the long corridor outside.

Orianna and Helen stood in the centre of the room. Helen's fingers were on the stopper of the glass vial. Orianna was holding the strands of Serrion's hair between her own fingers. As Helen upended the bottle a few sparks flew out. They drifted slowly down onto the hair. With a sudden crackling sound, a column of brilliant white light shot up into the air and a low humming sound began.

Orianna knew that Helen, as a member of the Select Families of Beltheron, had many gifts and talents allowing her to travel the pathways between worlds. She knew that Helen had successfully travelled between Beltheron, Earth and Atros several times in the past. As Helen held her hand out to her and she joined her in the column of light which was now filling the room, Orianna realised with a gulp that she herself was about to travel to Earth from Beltheron for the very first time.

'Don't worry,' Helen reassured her as they clasped hands and the light grew more blinding around them. 'We'll find Serrion.'

The light pulsed outwards and the humming grew to a deafening pitch. Then there was silence in the room. The column of light dimmed to a dull glow then blinked out. Helen and Orianna had disappeared. They had taken the pathway to Earth.

Green for Danger

Serrion, Adam and Joel had paused for breath on the street outside. The eyes of the two brothers were still full of questions, but Serrion began to take charge and talked to them rapidly, before they had chance to ask him anything.

'We need to get out of here, away from this place completely,' he said. 'If I am right about those two men then they are far more dangerous than you could ever imagine.'

He broke off as he raised his eyes and saw the figure of Bargoth, standing a short distance away, raising his weapon.

Serrion immediately flung his hand out towards Bargoth and started to yell a warning to his two friends.

Several things happened very quickly.

Adam's eyes followed Serrion's gesture and he turned in the direction of Bargoth and Heckle.

There was a crackle as a red bolt of energy shot from the end of Bargoth's gun.

The fire caught Adam on the shoulder as he turned in its path.

In the same instant of time the gate next to Lathe Heckle flew open – released by Serrion's outstretched hand – and crashed into him, making him stagger heavily into Bargoth. Serrion felt angry with himself, he had aimed for a direct hit on the assassin, but missed.

Joel screamed something as Adam fell to the ground.

Bargoth got off a second shot, but his aim was ruined by Heckle colliding with him.

The shot went wide and the windscreen of a parked car next to where the boys were standing exploded inwards.

'Come on!' screamed Serrion. He grabbed Adam's limp and whimpering form and hauled him to his feet. 'Can you walk?'

'Think so,' the poor boy was clutching at his shoulder and sniffling with a mixture of pain and shock.

'Walk? - my backside!' Joel yelled. 'We'd better *run!*'

The two brothers set off, Joel and Serrion supporting Adam as best they could. Serrion risked another look back at their pursuers.

Bargoth and Heckle were struggling to their feet. Before they could steady themselves however, a pale green light seemed to flash close by them and both men stiffened in pain then collapsed in a heap once more.

Serrion was startled. What had caused that? He noticed that Joel had seen the flash of green light as well. He looked at Serrion strangely as they raced away.

The three hurried back around the corner towards Serrion's old house.

'How did you do that?' Joel gasped as they ran.

'Yeah, that was amazin',' piped up Adam.

'I've never seen anything like it. How did you get them to just fall over like that?'

'What was that green light?'

'Was it a trick?'

'Are you a magician?' Both brothers laughed at this, Adam wincing with pain again as he did so.

Serrion didn't reply to any of their questions. That green light had had nothing to do with him. So who was it? Was it possible that there was someone else from Beltheron nearby? The questions turned over and over in his mind.

He ran on, his eyes focused for any strange movement on either side. He had to get back to the house. If Bargoth and Heckle had gone there, then there had to be a reason. They must have gone to the house to find something. Something important. But what?

He was confused by another image as well: the ransacked study in his old home. Someone else had got there before either Serrion or Bargoth and Heckle. Someone had already been looking in the house and had not worried too much about leaving tracks behind. Or they had been disturbed before they could tidy up again after themselves.

Serrion went cold at this thought. Had that unknown person - or persons - still been there in the house when he had arrived? Was *he* the one who had disturbed them?

In a moment he made his decision. He could waste no more time. Even though he was scared of what might be waiting for him there he knew that he had to get back to the house immediately.

Still holding onto Adam, they ran back down the road. As they approached the corner of the street that led to the house where the two brothers lived, Serrion stopped.

'Can you get your brother home by yourself?' he asked Joel.

'Uh huh, I think so,' the boy nodded.

'I must leave you here,' Serrion continued. 'Ring for an ambulance as soon as you get in. And get the police as well. Tell them there are two armed burglars breaking into houses on your street. Tell them they shot at you. That should deal with the two men chasing us – if they are still around. But whatever you do, don't mention me.'

'But what about all the…'

'Sorry, Joel,' Serrion's voice was firm. "You will just have to trust me. It is vital that you don't say anything about those flashes of green light, or doors flying open or anything like that.'

'But that was the best bit.' Joel looked sullen.

'I promise that I will come back and explain everything to you, but only if you both promise me to keep quiet for now.'

Neither one of the two brothers looked convinced. Here was an adventure they could amaze their friends with for weeks on end. It seemed unfair to have to keep it to themselves.

'Look, you told me that you liked stories, yes?' Serrion added. 'Well if you can keep this one secret for now, I can promise you the most fantastic tale you could imagine when I next see you.'

'Promise?' Adam asked.

Serrion nodded.

Adam looked across at his brother. They both considered for a moment, and then nodded together.

'Alright then,' Adam agreed. 'We'll be waiting. And it had better be good.'

'Thank you. Now you must get back home, ring for help and lock the door. Only open it again if it's the police, the ambulance or your mum and dad, ok?'

They both nodded again and Serrion hurried off down the street.

He got back to his old house without any further incident. Even so he checked behind him every few paces to make sure that he wasn't being followed. But there was no sign of Bargoth or Heckle. Perhaps they were still lying on the pavement, he thought. But what – or who - had caused that green flash of light?

Serrion walked up the path to the front door and raised his hand to open it. Suddenly a low humming sound filled the air and a flash of white light lit up the trees in the garden. Serrion shielded his eyes from the glare, but saw two familiar and very welcome shapes appearing in front of him.

The bright outlines of Orianna and Helen dimmed and then grew more solid as they materialised out of the pathway that Helen had created. Seeing him they both laughed out loud and ran towards him.

He grinned and ushered them quickly inside, all of them looking about them to make sure that their appearance had not been noticed by any passersby.

As soon as they were in the hallway Serrion closed the door behind them and locked it again with a flick of his hand. Then the greetings and questions began.

'Thank Council you're safe!'

'We came straight here to find you!'

'I'm glad you did.' Serrion replied. 'My vial got smashed in my rucksack. I wouldn't have been able to get back to Beltheron on my own.'

Helen held up her own vial. 'That's not a problem now,' she smiled. 'We can go straight back to Beltheron using this.'

'We'd better not be too long either,' Orianna grinned. 'Mum's got supper on the stove!'

Serrion smiled back at her. 'Alright, but I haven't been able to finish what I came here for yet.' He led them through to the ransacked study, explaining about what had happened as he went.

Both of the young women looked around at the wreckage of the room.

'Someone was very thorough here,' Orianna murmured.

'What were they looking for?' Helen asked.

'I don't know,' Serrion replied. 'And we can have no idea whether they found it or not.'

'But while we are here we might as well carry on

looking for any information that can be of help to us,' Orianna added decisively.

They began to wade through the papers and folders that were strewn over the floor and tables. They did not have a real plan in mind other than to find any news, letters, or objects that might lend a clue as to where the Andresens might be; something to hint at what they were planning. The chance to search through documents for clues and connections was too much for Orianna to resist and she was soon scurrying around, all thoughts of home and dinner far behind.

'They always used to lock the door to keep their important papers safe in here,' Serrion said. 'All the things to do with their 'business' as they used to call it.' He grinned to himself bitterly again. If only he had known at the time what that 'business' was all about.

'Well it could be anything or anywhere,' Helen complained as she lifted another heavy bundle of papers from the floor.

'It doesn't look as if this door has been forced in any way,' Orianna said. She had moved over to the study door and was looking at the handle and lock intently.

'Maybe it was Uncle Piotre or Aunt Sophia themselves,' Helen wondered. 'And maybe they ran off when they heard Serrion coming.'

But even as she said this she knew that it didn't make sense. Why would they have run from him?

'I'm absolutely certain that there must have been somebody else here,' Serrion replied.

'It could have been those two who were chasing you,' Helen suggested.

'Yes,' Orianna agreed. 'That's the simplest explanation.'

Serrion shook his head.

'No, they wouldn't have done that,' he said. Piotre

and Sophia were so keen on keeping that room private and secure. Those two who chased me were just grunts,' - Orianna smiled at this, she recognised the word as one that Parenon sometimes used to describe a dim-witted foot soldier – 'they wouldn't have been trusted with anything important.'

The three of them went back to their search in silence. They had been rummaging around without success for several more minutes when Orianna gave a cry of surprise.

'Here,' she cried. 'Now this could be very useful.'

Helen and Serrion walked over to her. She was holding a bundle of pale yellow papers fastened together in the corner with a strand of thin string. The pages were filled with small, densely packed writing, and a couple of them contained finely detailed hand-drawn diagrams. One of the pictures that Serrion could see over his sister's shoulder seemed to be of a large bird with a hooked beak. He shuddered and stepped back.

'It looks like Larena,' he said in a frightened whisper.

'It *is* Larena,' Orianna answered him. She was rifling through the other papers, quickly skim reading a few words here and there. 'These papers contain all the information that Piotre and Sophia used to allow her to change her shape into that horrible, hateful creature. Look, here are the incantations they used.'

She turned the sheets over to show one which was filled with strange shapes and symbols. 'This page gives us the runes that they would have carved onto the floor to change her in the first place.'

The other two looked to the places on the paper that she was pointing to.

'It's all here,' Orianna whispered excitedly.

She paused for a moment, deep in thought. 'If we study this properly,' she said slowly, as if to herself, 'it might give us the chance to change Larena back to her human form forever.'

'Are you sure?'

Orianna nodded.

'I'm positive. We could use this information to destroy her power.'

Serrion was still looking at the runes on the paper. There was something very familiar about the one in the centre of the page. It was circular, with something that looked like a black feather passing diagonally through it in one direction crossed by blue rippling lines that could have been water.

'I think I've seen this symbol somewhere before,' he murmured.

'Where?' asked Helen.

'I can't remember. But I know that it was quite a long time ago, before I lived on Beltheron.'

Orianna was still thinking carefully. 'If I am right, then the symbol would have been carved into the ground - or on the floor somewhere. Does that help, Serrion?'

He shook his head. 'Possibly, but nothing is coming to me at the moment.'

They carried on searching the papers and files but nothing else of interest caught their attention. Several minutes went by as they hunted.

'It could just be that the very thing we are looking for was taken by whoever got here before us,' Helen said in disgust. She was sitting cross-legged on a rug where she had been sifting through a pile of old bills. She spread her hands out, looking all around her at the floor. 'I can't find anything that gives us any hint where my aunt and uncle might have got to.'

After everything that she had discovered about Piotre and Sophia's betrayals and wickedness, Helen now had difficulty in thinking of them as her aunt and uncle. The very thought of them made her shudder at times.

However she was still happy to think of Serrion as her cousin. It did not matter to her that they had discovered the two of them were not really related after all. Even though she could not put it into words, Helen realised that the feelings and memories she had for him had not changed. Just because he was really Serrion Melgardes and not Jacques Andresen made no difference at all to what they had gone through together. She knew that it is what we feel for people in our own hearts and our shared experiences that really matter.

She looked up at him again. He was now standing very still and gazing at the rug she was sitting on.

'Orianna,' he said to his sister. 'You said this image would be carved on the floor somewhere?'

'That's right.'

'Well I think I've just remembered where I saw it. And I was right; it *was* years ago now, when I was little.'

Their eyes followed his. Helen suddenly got the point of what he was saying and scrambled to her feet. Together the three of them pushed back the piles of papers and books they had been studying and pulled away the heavy rug.

There on the floor was a series of runes and strange words. The image of the circle crossed by the black feather and rippling blue lines was featured prominently in the middle. Orianna gave a gleeful yelp of success and sank to her knees. She was already copying the words and symbols into a little leather-bound notebook, and murmuring under her breath.

'Landeyeda rabensmancer, Ragnorator et desolatum.'

'What does it mean?' Helen whispered.

'Old mythology, of some kind,' Orianna replied.

'I recognise some of the words from my studies, but I will have to check my ancient texts and ask the Cleve about it to understand it properly.'

Helen suddenly gave a cry of excitement and ran over to one of the book cases against the wall. It was the only one in the whole room that hadn't been disturbed.

'I think I saw those words, just a few minutes ago.'

She started looking along the shelves of books until she came to a row of several volumes that were all bound in the same dark purple leather.

'Here!' she shouted excitedly. 'This is it!'

The other two joined her. The spines of the books had old lettering on them in silver. The letters formed words that spread across the whole series of books.

Serrion began to read across the spines.

'The first one says 'Land', the second 'eye' and the third one 'darabens' and so on,' he said.

'But look,' Orianna interrupted. 'The last one must be missing. There isn't a book at the end with 'desolatum' on it.'

Sure enough, after the sixth book, which had 'toret' inscribed on the spine, there was a gap on the shelves. The space was perfectly obvious now that they were looking directly at it.

'That must be it,' Orianna said decisively. 'It ties in with the inscription on the floor, with Larena, with the writing in these papers.'

'Then it's no good spending any more time looking for it,' Serrion said. He gestured to the gap on the bookshelf. 'It's obvious that whoever ransacked this place found what they were looking for and took it.'

The others nodded in agreement.

'We should take the other books back with us too,' Helen said. 'Harrow might have a better idea about what's in the missing one if he can see the others.'

They gathered the purple books together and stuffed them into Serrion's ripped rucksack.

'I don't think that we're going to find anything else here tonight,' Serrion said. 'And my stomach's rumbling.'

'Yes, I'm afraid we'll already be dreadfully late for supper,' Orianna added. She grinned at the pair of them.

'This was far too important to miss though.' She was clutching her notebook tightly to her chest.

'I still wish I knew who had got here before us,' Serrion said.

'Someone sent by Piotre and Sophia?' Helen wondered.

'Or the two of them in person,' Serrion answered her with a cold flat tone to his voice. It made him feel very strange to think that the two of them might have been there only minutes before him.

'I don't think so,' Orianna said. 'They would have known what they were looking for and needn't have made such a mess everywhere.'

'And why send those other two thugs to the house straight afterwards?' Serrion concluded.

He was still thinking about that flash of green light. It had definitely helped him out of a dangerous spot. Could the person responsible for helping him in that way have been the same one who had ransacked the study?

He shook his head wondering about it.

'Anyway, we'll probably never know,' Helen said.

'You're right,' he agreed. 'Come on Helen, time to get that vial working. Take us back to Beltheron. Like I said before, I'm starving.'

Return to Beltheron

The three of them arrived in a swirl of white light and groaning rumbles that deposited them in the middle of Cleve Harrow's study. At the first sign of their appearance through the pathway he ran to his desk, and struggled to keep high piles of papers and old documents from being scattered around the room by the rushing wind created by their arrival.

'I wish that you would set your pathway to appear outside sometimes,' he said to Helen. 'Suddenly dropping into the middle of the room is very distracting.'

She realised he was only half serious, as she saw a twinkle in his yellowy-green eyes.

'If you think we're going to appear at the bottom of this tower and then walk all the way up those steps outside without even a handrail, then you have another thing coming!' she replied cheekily.

'I think that you will forgive us, Cleve, when you see what we have found,' Orianna added in an excited voice.

They told him about the ransacked room, the chase through the streets followed by the attack on Serrion, Adam and Joel, and then proudly told him of the scrawled messages and images they had discovered carved into the floor of Serrion's old house.

Orianna took out her notebook to show him the sketches and copies that she had made of the writing.

Harrow was immediately fascinated.

Serrion opened his rucksack and carefully lifted out the purple books with the silver lettering. As soon as Harrow saw these books his eyes widened in surprise for an instant. It seemed to Helen that he was about to say something and then changed his mind.

The Cleve looked at all of the books briefly, and then took a sheaf of papers from a deep fold in his robes. He began to scribble some notes onto them with a thin, black pencil. The others watched him in silence for several minutes, not wanting to interrupt his concentration. Soon he had filled three of four pages with small, neatly written text.

The Cleve folded the papers and took a small bar of red wax from another of his many pockets.

'A candle please, my dear,' he said as he gestured with his hand to Orianna.

She hurried to fetch one of the candles that was flickering on the window ledge. Harrow held the candle flame close to the block of wax and then placed the wax at an angle over the sheets of paper where the folded edges joined together. Serrion had seen him do this several times. He had even tried it himself once at school on Earth when he was younger. The class had been studying the Tudors and the teacher had wanted them to write letters to each other, sealed with wax in the same way that Henry VIII might have sent messages to one of his wives.

Harrow blew on the wax gently so that it cooled and hardened. When he was satisfied that the seal was complete and secure he handed the bundle to Orianna.

'Take this to Parenon tomorrow,' he said. 'This information that you have found needs to be shown to all of the pulver captains.' He smiled around at each of them in turn. 'Congratulations,' he beamed. 'You have achieved much that is important today.'

'I'm glad of that,' Helen said. 'But I've been thinking about something else. Why would my aunt and uncle still keep their house on Earth anyway? Wouldn't it have been safer just to move all their things to Atros?'

Harrow thought about this. He stared down at the ground for several moments. It was clear he was turning Helen's question over carefully.

'That is something I have asked myself as well,' he said finally. 'They always did have an arrogance about them. And maybe their advisers on Atros told them it was wise to keep their documents in different places, for security.'

Helen wasn't sure she agreed with the sense of this but Harrow had already changed the subject.

'I just heard a strange rumbling coming from Serrion's stomach,' he said. 'I think he'd be grateful to get home!'

'Mother's supper!' Orianna cried. 'We are so late, she'll be furious!'

'No more pathways in here today!' Harrow said quickly.

They made their hurried goodbyes to the Cleve and were soon racing – as quickly as safety would allow – down the treacherous staircase that led down the outside of the Cleve's tower.

Once they had reached the bottom, out of breath from the descent as usual, they hurried across the city.

Helen left them at the street corner that led to her own house just on the other side of the wide market square. Orianna and Serrion sped home.

When they arrived, Korellia was so relieved to see them that it overcame any anger she might have felt at their being so late.

'Come in, come in you two,' she fussed. 'It's getting

quite dark outside, I was getting dreadfully worried.' She pinched Serrion's cheeks affectionately.

'I lost you once, remember,' she said in a much more serious way. 'I couldn't bear to lose you again.'

'You needn't worry, Mother. We were together all the time.'

'Yes, but with that cursed crow woman here in Beltheron city itself…'

'But you know she is safe now, Mother,' Orianna interrupted. 'Trapped in the prison sphere that Jenia created.'

'Imprisoned is one thing – but she has killed, and she deserves to die herself!'

'Mum!' Serrion called out. He was shocked to hear his mother speak so violently – even about Larena.

'You're a good boy,' his mother replied. 'You have a kind, forgiving heart, in spite of everything you've seen and all the things that have been done to you. I know it's wrong, but I feel a vengeance in my heart about that, that… *thing.*'

They could see this was true. The cruelty that she felt towards Larena was obvious in Korellia's eyes as she glared around at them in defiance.

'Huh!' she murmured. 'Horrible shifting creature.'

'Beware of revenge,' Orianna said to her softly. 'It can destroy you from the inside and waste away your life as surely as if you were in your own prison. Larena has caused you enough pain. Don't let her have any further victory over you like this.'

There was silence between the three of them for a few moments. Only the crackling of the warm fire could be heard in the room. At last Korellia chuckled to herself.

'I'm sorry for being a foolish old woman,' she said to her children. 'Now come, get yourselves around that table.

The dinner has been keeping warm on the stove for far too long and it will be a miracle if it is not already ruined!'

Korellia was not the only one thinking of revenge.

On the world of Atros, it had been thundering all day. The skies were black with heavy, low clouds and the air itself seemed thick and wet. The ugly landscape was mainly made up of bare rock and shale that covered the low hillsides. There was no movement of person, animal or bird.

Then, as the rumbling in the air continued, a figure appeared from around the corner of one of the largest rocks. It was a man, terribly thin and ragged, and he carried a sack slung over one scrawny shoulder. The man was filthy. Grime covered his face and arms and dust from the ground mingled with traces of blood on his naked feet. He was a man that you might have felt some sympathy for if it had not been for the stream of vicious, violent curses that he spat almost continuously from his mouth. If you had heard those, then you would have shrunk away from him in fear and disgust.

As the man made his haphazard way across the barren landscape, another sound could be heard growing in the air. At first it was just like another element of the storm, a low humming underneath the grumbling of the clouds. But this sound grew in volume until the ground seemed to throb and shake. The man was startled and dropped his sack to the ground. A tall column of brilliant white light sprang up from the earth a few metres in front of him. The light changed to a deep blood red as the ragged man dropped to his knees in terror.

A figure stepped out from the column of red and moved purposefully towards the cowering man. The light dimmed around him until all that was left of it was a round scorch mark burnt into the earth.

He was a young man, really still only a boy of about fourteen or fifteen years. He had long, fair hair and was lean and muscled. He wore close-fitting riding breeches of leather, a silk tunic covered with a grey cloak and he carried a long, black staff in his right hand. The boy stood over the grovelling man and spoke in a clear, strong voice.

'Well, well. If it isn't my Master's old servant, Crudpile. It has been a long time since we last met.'

The man on the ground whimpered in new terror at the mention of his name.

'Who are you, sir? How do you know me and what do you want of me?'

'Look into my face! Don't say that you do not recognise me?'

The man on the ground raised his eyes and saw the boy's features for the first time. He gasped in sudden recognition.

'You! But I thought you were...'

'Dead? So did many others.' He began to laugh. 'But I am very much alive as you see.' His laughter became more manic and his voice grew louder with every word. 'Oh yes, it suited me and my parents to let people think that I had perished. But it takes more than a crumbling castle to kill me, and now I have returned! Yes, the mighty Jacques Andresen is here to begin his revenge!'

He turned away from the cowering form of Crudpile. As if he had suddenly had another thought Jacques stopped and turned back.

'You might be useful to us,' he said. 'If you want glory and reward, follow me.'

Crudpile whimpered again but was thinking quickly. It would be the best for him to stay in this young man's good books. And he *had* mentioned glory and reward.

Jacques was already walking away. Crudpile made his decision and began to follow him across the plain towards the ruins of Atros City...

Missed Opportunities

'That crazy bird-woman,' Korellia spoke to herself under her breath.

For the tenth time that day she thought; 'I don't care about what Orianna said about the dangers of revenge. I wish I could have five minutes alone with her. I would teach that hateful Larena a thing or two about revenge.'

She was making her way across Beltheron with her daughter at her side. It was late morning the day after Orianna, Serrion and Helen's adventure in London.

They were half way across the market square. The time tower gleamed in the morning sun. Its mirrors reflected the beams of light and created the shadows on the faces of the sundials that showed the correct time from any direction. Orianna glanced up at it: almost midday she realised.

They were late. Her mother had been fussing more than usual that morning, and several times they had been ready to go out of the door when Korellia had remembered something else that had to be done. Orianna now knew that she would have to go straight to Harrow's study in order to make her regular appointment with him. She did not want to miss any chance to study, particularly now, with so much new information being uncovered.

Inwardly though, she groaned. She had been looking forward to seeing Parenon so much this morning. It had been the only thing that she had been able to concentrate on for more than a moment at a time, in spite of the urgency of everything they were involved in. But even as the image of the young soldier rose in her mind again, she knew she would have to wait to see him.

'Mother,' she turned to Korellia. 'I am going to have to leave you for now. I must go for my meeting with the Cleve.'

Orianna fumbled in her leather bag. She drew out the sealed package of papers that Harrow had given to her the previous evening.

'It's very important that Parenon gets these today,' she said to her mother. 'Could you go to the great hall for me? He might be in one of the ante-rooms, or perhaps on the training field. It is Cannish's day to stand guard duty at the doors; he will be able to tell you where he is.'

Korellia nodded and took the bundle of papers from her daughter.

'Don't worry, my dear,' she soothed Orianna with the calmness of her voice. 'I will make sure your young man gets these.'

Orianna blushed suddenly. Had her mother just called Parenon *her* young man? She felt guilty, confused and embarrassed all at once. Could she have been so obvious? How had her mother guessed what she had been thinking and feeling about Parenon?

She risked a glance at her mother but there was no look of reproach or anger in her mother's eyes. Just love and understanding shone out at her. Orianna felt a rush of appreciation and affection for Korellia and held onto her hand for a moment longer. There was a silly tightness in her throat all of a sudden that made it awkward to speak.

She swallowed hard and managed to blurt out a couple of words.

'Thanks Mum.'

'Go,' Korellia smiled at her. 'You must see the Cleve.'

Orianna grinned in gratitude and clasped her mother's hand for a final brief moment.

She hurried away through the busy market place, without looking back. The sudden realisation of how much she loved her mother and what she meant to her was pushed to the back of her mind again as she began to think about the things she had to achieve that day.

If she had only known what the rest of that day had in store for her, and for all of them, she would definitely have looked back to smile and wave one more time.

Korellia watched her go. She followed her daughter with her eyes until she had disappeared among the stalls and brightly coloured flying machines that whipped past.

'My dear girl,' she thought. 'Do you know how proud I am of you, and how happy I want you and Serrion to be? I will take your papers to Parenon, and I will give him your very best wishes too, don't worry.'

She sighed and turned towards the side road that would take her up to the Great Hall and Ungolin's private quarters.

The Chamber

The chamber was freezing cold. The walls were carved smoothly from solid cold stone. In one dark corner the slow drip, drip, drip of water could be heard. The dripping noise was interrupted by the occasional low moan coming from a large figure chained to a metal chair in the middle of the room. The figure was human in shape, but the texture of its skin was unrecognisable. It was slick and smooth and at first glance the skin looked like wet metal. Muscles rippled under the surface. The figure twitched occasionally, a spasm running though its whole form making the chains clank and clatter.

Three people were standing around this metal chair. All three wore long dark cloaks and their attention was focused intently on the creature sitting there. These three were the people that had caused so much damage and hurt and worry. The ones who had lied, plotted and killed in the service of Gretton Tur, the Wild Lord of Atros.

They were Piotre and Sophia Andresen, and their son, Jacques. Three members of the Beltheron Select who had turned their backs on their friends and families in order to chase the evil glories and powers promised to them by Gretton Tur. Now, after his defeat and death, they continued to live in hiding in Atros City. Here, in the depths of what remained of Gretton Tur's old castle they continued their search for power, and plotted the ultimate destruction of Beltheron and Earth itself.

Piotre Andresen stepped forwards to the creature in the chair. It hissed at him as he drew closer, but the man did not flinch. He was not scared of this beast. He had no need to be for he had created it himself and he knew it might threaten, but would never actually harm its master. He raised his hand slowly to its slick features. Then, gently, he caressed its face. The creature's rage subsided until it was making a sound a little bit like a cat purring in contentment.

Piotre Andresen smiled. The smile narrowed his eyes into a cruel leer. He had a hard, angular face with broad cheek bones that stuck out sharply as if they were stretching the skin to breaking point. His wife stepped up to his side with a proud expression on her face and placed her hand lightly on his shoulder.

'My Beloved,' she whispered. 'Behold what greatness you have achieved.'

'Yes, my dark Queen,' he responded. 'Here is a servant to strike terror into those who would oppose us. Here is a brannoch, a foe that not even Ungolin's army could withstand.' He ran his hand over his wife's thin face and cupped her sharp chin in his long fingers. He bent to kiss her dark brown hair.

Behind them Jacques grinned malevolently. This would show that gutter boy Melgardes, and his own wretch of a cousin, the sickly sweet Helen, just how serious his family were about revenge and victory. He only hoped that he would be allowed to watch as his father's new creation killed them all.

His father and mother had both turned towards him. The creature behind them was still purring and grunting.

'Here is a great new gift for you, our son,' his father spoke proudly to him, his low voice curling like smoke around the room. 'Our pride and our partner in greatness, it is time for you to get to know your new pet.'

Jacques stepped forwards. He held out his hand to the creature in the chair. Like his father he was not scared by its open jaws or strange appearance. The creature sniffed and craned its neck as far forwards as it could while still chained tightly in the chair.

'Good boy,' Jacques cooed at it. 'There's a good boy.'

The creature growled again and began to lick his new master's hand. Its tongue was scaly and it scratched his skin, but Jacques was more than happy to let it continue. This was the best way for the animal to get to know him. It was obvious that it liked licking his hand.

Jacques took something out of his pocket. It was a small piece of cloth. He held it up to the brannoch creature's nose. Its nostrils widened as it began to sniff and salivate.

The snuffling sound gave way to a contented growling again, this time with a whimpering excitement, like a dog that has been offered a favourite treat and cannot wait for the food to be put into its bowl. Jacques took the cloth and placed it back into his pocket. The creature's excitement grew to fever pitch, it started bucking in the chair and the contented growling now turned into a frightening snarling wail.

'Be careful my son,' Piotre said with a note of laughter in his voice. 'You will get him too excited too soon. Besides, the brannoch has more urgent business to attend to on Beltheron before he begins to aid you in your search for revenge!'

Piotre pointed to the pocket where his son had placed the fabric moments before. 'Wait to show him these scraps of the Melgardes boy's shirt. Wait until you are in Beltheron city itself, and until the brannoch has caused his confusion and terror amongst the people. Then let your pet off his leash and watch him hunt!'

The three of them grinned at each other wickedly. As if by some invisible signal, father, mother and son all began to laugh together. As the sound of their glee grew in volume and intensity, the avid howl of Jacques' new 'pet', the brannoch, joined in and filled the cold stone chamber with its horrible sound.

Release and Revenge

Korellia walked into the training grounds past an ancient sign posted to a tree. Faded letters said 'Archery practice – keep clear!' as a warning. There were a few curling, yellowing leaves stuck to the sign, still wet from the rain of the evening before.

She had no difficulty in finding Parenon to deliver her daughter's message. He stood in the middle of the training field beyond the sign on the tree in the outer grounds of the Great Hall.

Vishan was at his side. They were dressed for combat and facing up to two other pulver running towards them.

'Hold steady! Hold steady!' called the Captain who was leading the exercise. 'Wait until they are closer.'

The men racing towards them suddenly drew their long gleaming swords and raised them over their heads. Parenon and Vishan remained motionless. Closer and closer the swordsmen came. At the last moment Parenon and Vishan spun to the side ducking away so that their attackers ran through a gap between them, stumbling in their haste. By the time the men had managed to turn around, and steady themselves, Parenon was holding a spear to the throat of one, and Vishan brandished a bow, notched with an arrow that pointed straight at the belly of the second. There was absolute stillness for one moment, then all of the men roared out loud with laughter.

'Well done you two!' the Captain shouted. 'Perfect timing!'

'Nice work Vishan,' the older of the two attacking pulver said.

'I can never get one over on you,' the second grinned at Parenon.

'Take a break for fifteen minutes,' the Captain said.

The men slapped each other on the back and began to unsling their training gear.

Parenon looked up and saw Korellia walking across the training ground towards them. He raised his hand to wave. He was fond of the old woman and even fonder of her beautiful daughter.

He blushed red as he thought of Orianna.

'Foolish idiot!' he thought. 'As if someone like her would even think twice about a soldier like me.'

Korellia waved back at him. He excused himself to Vishan and began to walk towards her.

'Good day, my lady,' he said in greeting.

'Parenon, my friend, I hope I am not taking you from your work?'

'A break is very welcome. The Captain has been working us hard this afternoon.'

'I have brought you a message.' Korellia's eyes twinkled with mischief as she spoke. She looked carefully at Parenon's face to catch his reaction to the thought of news from Orianna. She was not disappointed. Deep in his eyes there was a sudden gleam of excitement, and he grinned as he bit his bottom lip. 'Like a six year old waiting for ice cream,' thought Korellia.

'A message?'

'She would have brought it herself, but needs to see the Cleve.' Korellia began to take the papers out of her bag. 'Orianna and the Cleve were sure that these were important. They thought that you could look at them first, and then show the rest of the pulver what they found.'

She noted that there was a slight shadow of disappointment on Parenon's face that the message wasn't of a more personal nature, but it faded quickly. In a moment he was the businesslike soldier again.

'Of course, anything that I can do to help.'

Parenon broke the Cleve's red wax seal and began to scan the papers. Then he moved onto Orianna's own pages. His eyes roved quickly over her small, neat handwriting.

'She and the Cleve found information in one of her old texts,' he said as he scanned the writing.

'It talks about the nature of shape shifting that allows Larena to stay as a bird for such a long time without draining her own energy,' he continued speaking as he reached the bottom of the first page. He glanced up and down the writing once more, deep in thought.

'Orianna writes here that both she and the Cleve thought that all the pulver guards should see the symbols they found, in case any of us finds or recognises similar signs anywhere else.

'Our friend, the rebel Tarawen, is busy on Atros. He has been watching the movements of the rish for us recently,' Parenon continued. 'A group of my men are about to go on a mission to Atros to try to seek out the few remaining bands that he has discovered.'

He gestured to the papers in his hand.

'These new discoveries could be extremely helpful to them too. I will pass this information onto my guards in the pulver straight away. They must remain alert to any clue however small it may seem.'

'I think that you are right,' Korellia replied. 'This is surely important for both Orianna and the Cleve to become so excited.'

Parenon nodded in agreement. He took two or three sheets of paper from the rest. Then he bundled the remaining pages back together and handed them to Korellia.

'You must take the rest of these pages to Lord Ungolin straight away. Ungolin has been visiting the Birdwoman a lot recently with Harrow, Jenia and Matthias. There is much discussion going on as to how to finally deal with her.'

Korellia had stiffened at the mention of Larena. The hateful Birdwoman again! Would she never break free of her connections with that creature? She hid her anger though, as she nodded in agreement with Parenon and took the papers back from him.

'Very well, thank you for your advice. I will take these straight to them.'

She turned and walked purposefully back across the training ground towards the towers of Ungolin's chambers.

Cannish was still on duty at the door to the staircase, just as Orianna had expected. He stood to attention when he saw Korellia approach.

'Welcome my Lady,' he said in greeting.

'Cannish, good day to you. Is Ungolin present?'

'He is at his meal, and probably best not disturbed right now.' Cannish gave a grin. Even though everyone recognised Ungolin to be a kind hearted and patient man, Cannish knew that he had spent a long morning in consultation with Jenn and Matt, and how tetchy he could get if he were kept from his lunch for too long. Cannish had been on the wrong end of Ungolin's short temper once too often.

Korellia smiled back. She understood his meaning perfectly.

'And Jenia, or Matthias?'

'Gone back home not twenty minutes ago.'

'Very well,' Korellia continued. 'Could you tell Lord Ungolin that I have important papers from my daughter and Cleve Harrow that he will be interested in? I will leave them in his study on his desk.'

'Of course.'

He opened up the heavy oaken door and Korellia began to climb the winding staircase.

'I shouldn't be too long,' she called back to Cannish.

She had soon reached Ungolin's room. Korellia had been there on a couple of occasions in the past, when Cleve Harrow had discovered how important and clever a student her daughter was, and had taken her to be introduced to the Lord. This was the first time she had entered the ancient chamber by herself however and she shivered slightly at the cold breeze that blew down the hall towards her as she pushed open the door.

The room was lit by a thin beam of mid afternoon sun which broke through a high window. It illuminated old desks and high backed chairs which Ungolin found the most comfortable for relaxing and reading. Tall bookshelves filled the far wall opposite Korellia as she entered.

Her eyes immediately began to search along the shelves. After just a few moments she saw it. There, among the dusty volumes and old scrolls glimmering in the soft light was a large glass ball. A quick glance at it from most people would have revealed nothing more than an oversized paperweight. But if you looked more closely, even from across the other side of the room then you might become aware of a slight movement inside.

Again, others might mistake this movement for a trick of the light or their own eyes deceiving them, but Korellia knew better. She knew full well what was actually contained inside that glass ball. It had been dominating her thoughts for long enough.

With grim determination she stepped swiftly across the room. She stood by the shelf, her face now only centimetres from the sphere. Inside was the focus of so much of her hatred and anger. There, trapped within the glass walls was the figure of a woman – shrunk to the size of a small bird – dressed entirely in black. As Korellia stared the woman's tiny face snarled at her and stuck out a pointed black tongue.

'Larena,' whispered Korellia with a cold hard edge to her voice. 'At long last we come face to face. I have waited so long for this moment.'

The small bird-woman in the globe was motionless now; her gaze fixed steadily upon the older woman.

With a sudden movement, Korellia lunged for the globe. It was heavy – much heavier than she had expected from its size - and it took all her strength to lift it but she was spurred on by an insane rage. Raising it high above her head she dashed the globe to the hard stone floor.

The shock of the impact broke the defensive power that Jenn and Harrow had created in the globe. It shattered into thousands of tiny pieces that began to smoulder immediately with a thick dark grey smoke.

Korellia lifted her foot; ready to stamp upon what she thought must be a defenceless, bird-sized Larena. But before she could see her target through the now billowing smoke, a terrifying laugh sounded from the ground. The laugh was half cackle, half choke, and it made Korellia's heart turn cold with an overwhelming fear.

Her foot was still raised and ready to fall when there was a bright flash of white light. Korellia tried to shield her eyes but it was too late, she had been momentarily blinded. By the time her vision began to clear again, Larena was back to her full height and standing in front of her.

'Fool!' she hissed. 'You thought you could defeat me? How little you know of my power.'

Korellia gave a whimper of fear mingled with rage and struck out with her fist at Larena's harsh face.

Quick as a flash, Larena raised her own hand and grasped Korellia's in a tight grip. Korellia was shocked at the speed and strength of her adversary. She had hardly even seen her move. Larena's other hand leapt to Korellia's throat, making her gasp.

The fingers began to tighten around Korellia's windpipe. She was now struggling to get her breath. Larena slowly lifted the older woman up off the ground, until she was suspended several centimetres in the air.

Larena's strength was frightening. Korellia began to panic and struggle. She still could not get her breath. Larena's fingers were like a strong vice at her throat. She was staring deep into her eyes with an evil glint that made her victim quail with terror. There was not a trace of pity in those dark eyes, just vindictive pleasure.

'You know I *had* to kill your husband,' her words now were meant to add additional pain.

'My Darion?' Korellia croaked. '*Why*? Why couldn't you just stay away from my family?'

'He was guarding Ungolin in the Great Hall,' Larena said. She spoke more slowly now, as if she had all the time in the world. Korellia still dangled in her grasp.

'Sophia came into the room carrying your son after we had taken him and started to use him to cover up Jacques's disappearance. Of course, your husband recognised his own baby son instantly. He didn't say anything but Sophia saw the look in his eyes, she saw him start with surprise and the slow cogs of his mind beginning to turn on what had happened. We knew right then that we had to dispose of him before he could reveal our plans.'

'You killed him for *that*!'

'He was of no importance to us! Hah! A mere pulver guard? He was a nobody! He was a sacrifice that it was easy to make!'

'He was a good man,' Korellia gasped through her choking tears. 'A good, brave man. He was my husband and I loved him.'

'Weak, so weak!' Larena cackled. 'You are all ruled by your petty emotions. That is your failing. That will be the eventual undoing of you all. Your silly love and affections for each other will bring about your everlasting defeat.'

As she said these final words, Larena's fingers tightened once more. With a last convulsive gasp, Korellia slumped to the ground.

The black figure of Larena crouched over the still form of Korellia. Then, slowly at first, she began to change.

Her hands - which were still at Korellia's throat – began to grow darker and stiff feathers started sprouting from the fingernails. These feathers multiplied and began to split the black cloak apart. It fell to the ground in rags and pieces as her head shrank back into her neck and her eyes grew smaller and rounder. Her long hooked nose transformed into a sharp beak. With a brittle, cracking sound her legs turned grey and sharp talons sprang from the ends of what had been her feet.

Flapping her wings, Larena jumped onto Korellia's body and with a sickening ferocity began to peck and claw at the dead woman, occasionally holding her sleek black head to the roof and cawing with gleeful triumph.

On and on she ripped and stabbed until her feathers were slick with red. Now her eyes shone with delight and satisfaction.

'Father and mother have both fallen to me,' she hissed to herself. 'And soon their children will also be my victims.'

Her small, dark, hard bird's tongue flicked in and out as if licking her beak.

At long last the horrible work was done. With a flap of her wings, Larena rose up into the air and flew to the window. There were long, dark clouds the colour of bruises beginning to stretch across the blue skies above Beltheron City.

With a single stab from her beak Larena shattered the window, the fragments of glass tumbling away below her to the bottom of the tower. A number of Ungolin's guards looked up and began to run around, dodging away from the falling shards. They shouted instructions and warnings to each other as they saw the figure of the large bird hovering in the window frame.

These guards did not worry Larena though. With a high cawing cry she spread her black wings in freedom and victory. Again and again she called to the darkening sky.

Then, her cries were answered. Faintly at first, but then growing in number and volume, as more and more birds began to reply. Sparrows and finches twittered from under the eaves of cottages; blackbirds and magpies swooped down from chimneys, singing through the streets; crows and ravens like smaller versions of herself cawed excitedly from the trees in the distant parks of the city; and high, high up, circling majestically in the warm thermal winds far above the tallest rooftops, the wide-winged hawks and harriers answered the dread call of Larena the Birdwoman.

The sound grew throughout the city. People rushed from their homes into the streets with anxious, questioning expressions on their faces. They pointed upwards and shouted warnings to each other as they saw the birds. Some were scared by the sight, others were excited, and a few just laughed with delight at the unusual spectacle above their heads.

Soon the cawing, calling and shrieking had reached a deafening level. Those who had run outside now returned home and slammed their doors. Even those who had enjoyed the sight as an interesting natural phenomenon now shook their heads in fear and wonder and hurried back inside. Windows were closed and shutters brought down. Children huddled in the corners of their rooms, hands pressed tightly over their ears. And still the sound grew.

The sun was still quite high in the sky but even so the air was beginning to grow dark. The flurry of hundreds of thousands of birds filled the air, blocking out the light.

Larena still perched in the window frame of the tower, calling to her new army. She could hear the footsteps of guards coming up the stairwell behind her but she didn't even turn around to look.

Cannish was in the lead as the guards reached the door and he gasped in horror as he saw the crumpled body of Korellia. But even as Cannish and his companions drew their weapons to aim at the huge bird in the window she gave one relaxed flap of her mighty wings and flew up into the skies.

Far below her, the streets and buildings of Beltheron City were plunged into darkness by a million wings.

Dangerous Flight

Serrion had been spending the afternoon with Helen, Matt and Jenn. They were all seated around a large table with the remains of a large feast scattered around them. Jenn had always been a fantastic cook, Serrion remembered. She used unusual ingredients to flavour her dishes, and some things found their way into her bubbling pots and pans that most people would never even have considered as food. Under her masterful skills however, everything always tasted delicious. Even when she prepared a small snack for him and Helen to take with them it was always sustaining and filled him like a hearty three-course dinner. Now, after one of her magnificent full meals inside him he sat back with a satisfied grin on his face.

'Come, Serrion,' Matt said. 'It's our turn now, pick up those dishes next to you and come and help me with the clearing up.'

They were just beginning to tidy away some of the bowls when Serrion's attention was caught by a candle in the middle of the table. It sputtered and flickered as it neared its end, but instead of the light growing dimmer, it flared up in a bright, red flash. Serrion shook his head. He blinked a couple of times but the red glow was still there. He knew by now that he could not ignore such a sign.

'Uncle Matt,' he began, 'I think that something is about to…'

Before he could finish speaking there was a loud crack at the window. They all jumped and looked out.

The glass had been smashed near the centre. There was a circular crack, with other cracks spreading out towards the edges of the window, like jagged spokes on a wheel.

Helen was already running towards the door.

'Wait!' Jenn cried out. 'You don't know what's out there!'

Helen was too excited to stop. She threw the door open and looked down at the ground underneath the window.

'Oh! That's odd.'

'What is it?' Serrion was quickly at her side, with Matt and Jenn not far behind.

They all looked down at the ground. There lay the broken body of a bird. It was the size and shape of a magpie, but with yellow in place of black feathers. Its head was held back at a strange angle and both feet stuck up into the air.'

'Poor creature,' Jenn said. 'It mustn't have seen our window.'

'Yes it is getting strangely dark,' Matt answered. They all looked up to the sky, to see if rain clouds were gathering. Overhead they saw dozens of birds all flying in the direction of Ungolin's palace.

'That *is* strange,' Serrion whispered. 'I wonder what's spooked them?'

There were now more and more birds filling the patch of sky that they could see above the roofs of the houses on their street. A cacophony of cawing, hooting and whistling began to grow in the air.

Matt was bending down to look more closely at the bird on the ground. His wife's voice stopped him before he could pick it up.

'Wait,' she said. 'Don't touch it Matt.'

All four of them exchanged worried glances as the birdsong around them grew louder.

'This isn't right,' Jenn said. 'Get indoors, quickly!'

Parenon had been showing the other pulver the information that Korellia had given to him. They were gathered around a long oak table in the middle of the hall in their training quarters. Light shone down diagonally from tall windows set deep into the heavy thick stone walls. The slanting light shone on the bundle of papers that Parenon was holding.

'So, on your trip to Atros you must keep your eyes alert for any sign or symbol similar to this one,' he instructed them. 'We never know how it might be of use, to the Cleve and Orianna,' he continued.

The others all nodded and murmured words of assent. They each knew the importance of the work that they did, and how vital it was to the safety of the land they loved so much.

'Thank you men,' Parenon concluded. 'I believe I may now release you from your duties for the rest of the aftern...'

'Parenon!'

Cannish ran into the hall as Parenon was speaking.

All the guards turned, some reaching for their swords in alarm. They stopped and gazed in astonishment at their breathless companion.

Cannish's tunic was ripped in many places, and trickles of blood ran down the pale fabric. Cannish held his sword in one hand, but it drooped down to the floor. There was one particularly livid gash above his left eyebrow and he had to blink continuously to keep the blood from dripping into his eye.

Parenon leapt towards him, pushing the other guards out of the way.

'My friend, what has happened to you?'

'The Birdwoman,' Cannish managed to gasp through clenched teeth. 'She has escaped, and, and...'

Tell me!' Parenon was by his side now. His hand was under Cannish's elbow, supporting the breathless pulver.

'She has escaped,' Cannish repeated. 'And the demon has released a great evil! The birds... the birds are attacking!'

Even as he spoke they heard a terrifying sound from outside the hall. A keening, wailing sound like dead spirits pleading for forgiveness.

'To the doors!' Parenon yelled, 'Let us see what wickedness has now been released upon us!'

Eight or nine of the pulver guard ran immediately to the large doors where Cannish had appeared less than a minute ago. They pulled the wide double doors apart. All now had their swords or daggers in their hands, ready for immediate action.

But even the most experienced of the pulver quailed in fear at the sight that met them. Before Parenon had chance to rally his men with an order to fall into battle formations, a host of crows, ravens and huge hawks with wide wings descended from the skies...

High, high up above Beltheron City, Larena soared on the updrafts of warm air. She gazed out beneath her as her bird army swooped and plundered the houses and streets. Her small, dark, cruel eyes glinted with delight and victory as she heard the screams rise up towards her on the air.

A raven with ragged black feathers flew up towards her.

'Mistress, what do you command?' it croaked as it flapped in front of her.

'Cause as much confusion as you can in the streets and the houses,' Larena replied. 'Then we wait.'

'What are we awaiting, O Great One?' it cawed.

'Soon our Master and Mistress will be here,' Larena answered. 'Piotre and Sophia Andresen will arrive and lead us all to a great victory.'

The Worst Possible News

Orianna and Harrow had been deep in concentration at their books for over an hour. Even though they had found out lots of important information over the last twenty-four hours, there were still mysteries about exactly what Larena's shape shifting powers might be.

They were pulling another set of old volumes from a high shelf in one corner of Harrow's study when they heard the first of the bird calls. For a few moments they ignored it, but the sound outside began to grow more and more insistent.

'What is going on out there?' Orianna muttered to herself. She walked towards one of the windows. 'It sounds as if someone has attacked a nest and every bird in Beltheron is calling out for... Oh!'

She had reached the window and her jaw dropped as she gazed out.

Harrow looked up from the book he had just opened.

'What is it my dear? You sound worried. I know that those birds have begun to make a dreadful noise but...'

'Cleve, I think you should come and look at this.'

He made his way to stand behind her at the window and followed Orianna's gaze.

The sight that met his eyes made him freeze with horror.

From the high vantage point at the top of his tower

they could see innumerable birds wheeling around in the sky above and below them; birds of every breed, size and shape. So far it seemed that the crazed birds had not noticed them, but as they watched a particularly large starling hurtled towards them, its speckled feathers glinting in the light. They both jumped back in alarm as it hit the window with a thud and then tumbled slowly away towards the ground far below, its neck broken.

'This is not normal behavior,' Harrow said (rather unnecessarily Orianna thought). 'There is an evil working here through these creatures,' he muttered.

Orianna was still looking down, following the falling path of the dead starling when she gasped again.

Coming up the open stairs around the outside of the tower was Parenon. His sword was in his hand and he was fending off the birds as best he could as he struggled upwards. Twice as she watched she thought that he must fall, and her hand shot to her mouth to stop her crying out in alarm.

But Parenon kept his balance on the uneven stairs. Even as a flock of starlings dive-bombed him with their sharp, jabbing beaks he twisted into the wall, protecting his head by covering it with his pale blue cloak and swiping at them with his sword.

He was closer now. There were only a few more steps. He had almost reached the door. Harrow was waiting to open it as soon as he got there.

But with just one or two more steps to go, a kite with a massive wingspan wider than an adult man's outstretched arms swooped down. It plucked at Parenon's cloak. The huge bird of prey had appeared so suddenly that Orianna did not even have time to scream out a warning.

The bird had great strength and succeeded in pulling Parenon off balance. He tottered at the edge of the topmost step as the kite continued to harry him with its talons.

Without pausing to think, Orianna hurled herself across the room to the door. She slipped under Harrow's arm and pulled open the door of the study.

'Orianna, wait!'

But it was too late to stop her; she was already outside on the ledge next to the top step. Orianna began to call out to distract the bird's attention.

'Over here! Heeagh! Heaagh!' she cried.

It worked. The kite pulled up and away on a draft of warm air, leaving Parenon still staggering at the edge of the long drop. It wheeled around in the air above Orianna's head, searching for the best place to strike out at this new, unexpected adversary. The bright patterns of red and gold underneath its outstretched wings filled the whole of Orianna's vision for a moment as it began to dive towards her. Then she felt the breath pushed out of her body as Parenon hurled himself into her and pushed both of them back through the open door. Harrow slammed it closed and they heard a loud '*whump*' as the kite hit the other side.

Parenon and Orianna had fallen in a heap on the floor.

'I am sorry, my Lady,' Parenon began. 'I… I… I did not mean to hurt you.'

He was struggling to get up to his feet and help Orianna at the same time. She couldn't help giggling at how embarrassed he was.

As soon as they were both standing again however, the look on his face made the laughter dry up in her throat.

'Sorry Parenon, I shouldn't laugh. What is happening with the birds? Why are they attacking like this?'

'Is it happening all over the city?' Harrow continued. He was still at the window, staring intently at the incredible scenes outside.

Parenon did not reply at first. He gazed at the ground

in front of him, unable to look up and meet their faces. Eventually he managed to speak.

'Yes, Cleve,' he began. 'The attacks are happening all over Beltheron. The Birdwoman, Larena, has escaped.'

'What?'

'Oh no,' Orianna interrupted. 'I thought she was secure. Parenon, how could she…'

Parenon raised his hand to silence their questions. He took a deep breath and finally looked Orianna directly in the eyes.

'Your mother went to Ungolin's chamber where Larena was being kept prisoner. No one knows exactly what happened, but somehow the glass sphere that held Larena was broken. She… she…'

A slow, dreadful realization began to seep into Orianna's mind. Even as Parenon struggled to find the right words to tell her, Orianna was thinking about her recent conversations with her mother about the hated Birdwoman. She remembered her mother's fury and desire for revenge. The expression on Parenon's face only served to increase her fear.

'My mother,' she said quietly. 'Tell me what has happened to my mother.'

'Larena attacked her,' Parenon said simply. 'There was nothing that anyone could do. By the time the guards got to the room, Larena had… She had… Your mother was…'

His words were interrupted by Orianna's sudden sobbing. She had guessed the worst. She collapsed forwards and Parenon stepped towards her to catch her in his arms.

'I'm so sorry,' he whispered into her white hair. 'So, so sorry.'

Harrow stood behind them silently. His face was grim. He allowed the two young people just a couple of minutes to comfort and be comforted. Then he cleared his throat loudly. Difficult as it was, Harrow knew that there was no more time to be spent like this. He had to take action.

'My dears,' he spoke softly, kindly. 'This is terrible; the worst possible news.'

He lifted his arms to Orianna, and hugged her tightly, even as she carried on clutching at Parenon's hands.

'You need time to be alone, time to grieve,' he continued. 'But most of all now you need to get to safety.'

'No, I must go to her,' Orianna sobbed.

'There is nothing that you can do for her,' Parenon replied sadly. 'She is gone.'

'It is too dangerous here in the city,' Harrow added. 'You must leave.'

He looked Orianna directly in the eyes. 'My dear, I know it is no comfort to you right now, but you must know that I care for you very deeply, and I will do all in my power to keep you safe.'

He turned to Parenon. 'The best way to do that is to place her in your care for now. You must get her away from here. Quickly!'

Of course Cleve,' the pulver replied. 'It is my honour and privilege to do so. But where will we go? Where *can* we go where Orianna will be safe?'

'I will help,' Harrow said. 'I have an idea. You must leave Beltheron City immediately. I will create a pathway for you.'

'Can we not take the golden staff ourselves?'

'No. I am afraid that I will need it very much more than you in the coming days. Do not worry. I will send you somewhere no one will find you.'

'But what about Serrion?' Orianna said through her tears. 'I can't just leave my brother. He must be told.'

'I will go to him,' the Cleve said.

'You will tell him what has happened?

'I will do all I can. You must not worry about him now. Think about your own safety.'

Orianna looked from Cleve Harrow to Parenon and back again. She knew, painful as it was, that he was right.

'Look after Serrion for me,' she said in a broken voice. 'Tell him I love him, and to keep himself safe.'

He nodded. 'Fear not, I will make sure that your brother is safe.'

Harrow turned to Parenon. 'Things are changing faster than any of us could have imagined.' The Cleve spoke rapidly. 'We need to work together to defeat this new evil but, for the time being at least, we are all safer - and stronger - if we part company.'

Parenon nodded in understanding and agreement.

'There is no more time for talking,' Harrow continued. 'You have to get her away now. I charge you with her care Parenon. She is most important. Protect her. Do not fail me in this, Captain of the Pulver.'

'Sir, I will not.'

Harrow was already rummaging in a wooden chest in one corner of his room. He brought out a small vial of dark liquid and pressed it into Parenon's hand. He then crossed the room rapidly and took a slim volume from a shelf. He gave the book to Orianna.

'Words of comfort for you my dear, blessed Orianna,' he said. 'Read this when you are at your most troubled. I know how much you trust in the power of words, and the ones contained in this book will bring some relief.'

Harrow thought for a moment, as if he had suddenly remembered something, but wasn't sure whether to mention it or not. Then, with a quick nod of his head, he made his decision. He took the book from Orianna again and began flicking through the pages. The Cleve found what he was looking for and turned the open book towards Orianna.

'Here,' he said, pointing with his finger. 'Read and remember these lines. You will need them.'

She looked down. Harrow was pointing at an old incantation. It was written in swirling letters of fading ink.

'Why do I need this?' she asked. 'How do you know it is important?'

'I have no time to explain,' he replied. 'But learn it anyway. I believe it to be connected to the symbols which you found at the Andresen's house on Earth. This book is very important.'

'He turned back towards Parenon.

'Not only that,' he said, 'but sprinkling a few drops of liquid from that bottle onto the book will bring you straight back to this room if you should need to.'

Parenon nodded, he understood perfectly.

'Wait for at least two days,' Harrow said. 'Unless you hear from me that it is safe, do not return before then. Now go my friends!'

With these last words he raised the staff high over his head and a column of white light sprang up around Parenon and Orianna. As the light deepened to a thick, blood red and a familiar humming, droning sound filled the room, the two of them vanished.

Harrow was left alone in his study. The light from the pathway dimmed and disappeared. Outside, the sound of the birds continued.

The End of Tarawen's Waiting

It was late afternoon on the third day of waiting by the time they arrived.

It started with a low dust cloud on the hill, dust that had been raised from the dry floor of Atros by the tramping of many hooves and feet.

By now, even Tarawen's attention had begun to fade. He had slept lightly on and off during the nights, and every hour or so he had allowed himself to move position. When he was absolutely certain that no one was nearby he stood and walked around for a couple of minutes just to keep his muscles moving.

But now it was all he could do to keep his eyes open.

Tarawen shook his head to clear his thoughts from the sleepy fug that he had almost allowed himself to fall into. Once more he shifted his grip on his sword.

He had been expecting only a handful of rish, and maybe a couple of holva steeds at most. But the increasing size of the dust cloud made it apparent that there was a huge number approaching. He huddled down further into hiding. There was no way that he could challenge such large numbers by himself.

The crowd drew ever closer to where he was hiding. He could see them clearly now. The motley group was being led by three proud figures riding on the backs of their jet black holva.

Tarawen recognised these three riders immediately. Piotre, Sophia, and Jacques Andresen. Jacques! But that was impossible! Surely he had perished in Tur's castle! Tarawen shook his head in disbelief and carried on watching.

Piotre Andresen was a tall man with a hard angular face and piercing blue eyes. He held the long black staff of Atros proudly in his right hand.

Sophia, his wife, stared imperiously around her at the gathered troops. She wore a long velvet cloak of deep purple. She had a calm expression on her beautiful face that was surrounded by cascades of flowing dark brown hair. Their son Jacques just grinned wickedly at all this new excitement.

As the trio brought their steeds to a halt, the crowds of rish gathered around them. There were over fifty of them altogether. Some carried black flags with rough, red lettering that Tarawen did not recognise. In one of their other three arms, they gripped swords, cruel looking spears with jagged hooks on them, and other vicious weapons. Their final two hands were used to hold the reins that were fastened through the holva's cheekbones with spikes.

They were only a few metres away from where Tarawen was hiding and he shivered in fear of being seen.

He kept deadly still, even slowing down his breathing as if the air might be heard on his lips. The clanking of the rish's own armour and rattling of the weapons in their many hands was too loud for that to happen though. They were so close to his crouching, hidden form that Tarawen's immediate worry was not of being seen or overheard, but of being trampled underfoot be one of the holva, or tripped over by one of the rish themselves. He could smell their rank flesh and it made his own skin crawl with distaste and revulsion. Such horrible creatures!

There were a couple of shambling characters moving

along in the midst of the rish and other Atrossian men that Tarawen thought he recognised.

Both wore brightly coloured jackets – although these were torn and had been patched and re-patched from several sources – and baggy breeches tucked into long, muddy boots.

'Crudpile and Dross!' Tarawen thought sullenly as he finally managed to put a name to these faces. 'I had hoped never to see those two villainous thugs again.'

Over the years, Crudpile and Dross had had many dealings with the rebels who Tarawen worked with on Atros. On every occasion that their paths had crossed, Tarawen had been reminded of the cruelty and small minded greed of these two villains.

True to form, the pair were arguing as they marched along.

'Oi don't see why we had to come along anyway, Crudpile,' Dross was complaining.

'Shut it!' Came the reply.

'But why?'

'Don't argue. We're obeying orders.'

'My feet hurt.'

'Yeah, and they stink as well, but you don't hear me complaining.'

'No good'll come of this, Crudpile.'

'And no good would have come to us if we'd just stayed put in Atros City. Here at least we have a chance for glory and reward.'

Crudpile now lowered his voice so he wouldn't be heard. 'And we might even get our chance to escape. When everyone else is fighting and too busy watching their own backs we can sneak away.'

Dross grinned wickedly.

'Now that's more like the Crudpile I know!' he said.

'I was beginning to think that you had gone all soft in the head.' He laughed loudly.

'Shut it I said!' Crudpile replied. 'Keep up the pretence of followin' the Andresens and the rest o' this mob and we might just get the chance of a sweet life when we get to Beltheron City.'

The rest of the conversation was lost as Crudpile and Dross were shuffled off in the pack of men and rish.

'Beltheron City!' Tarawen thought to himself. 'They are going to attack Beltheron!' He tucked himself even further down into his hiding place.

The crowd had stopped now however, and were all concentrating on their leaders. Some distance away Piotre Andresen looked around at them all. There was a wicked leer across his face.

'My worthy friends, noble warriors,' he shouted to the crowds. 'Now is the time that many of you have been waiting for. For too long you have suffered through the work of the aged fool Ungolin. Our lands have been ripped from us by the greed of the Beltheron attackers. Your homes and your food have been ransacked and robbed.'

There were grunts and yells of anger and agreement at what Piotre Andresen was saying. He knew that he had their sympathy and full attention. He also knew exactly what to say to influence their simple loyalty and raise their bloodlust to fever pitch.

Tarawen had been edging himself around the edge of the group carefully so that he could remain within sight of the speaker. He managed to get to a safe spot behind a tussock of tall grass in time to hear Piotre's voice rise even higher in indignant fury.

'For far too long many of you have waited patiently for justice. Well now the waiting is over and at last that justice is here!'

He raised his hands wide in the air as he spoke his final words. 'Now we can bring the destruction to Beltheron that we have longed for. Now, after much patient study and work, we can all travel the pathway together. Who will join me in our triumphant hour?'

There was a deafening cheer. It was clear that every one of the nightmarish creatures would follow Piotre Andresen to victory or to their doom. In their violent fury it wasn't clear if they even minded which one it turned out to be.

Piotre raised the black staff once more. The raucous cheering was immediately silenced. Sophia raised herself even more proudly in her saddle. Jacques leered and licked his lips in expectation of his father's next words.

'At long last we have found success in our studies,' Piotre continued. 'We have discovered the secrets of the old magics and spells.'

There was another cheer, even louder than the first – if that were possible.

'Even after his death our great and noble Lord, Gretton Tur, has found a way to reveal all to us in his books.'

'He has shown us the secret,' Jacques butted in, unable to stop himself any longer. 'My father has found the way to take us all to Beltheron together, so join us and take your orders from us!'

Piotre placed his hand on his son's shoulder to restrain him. Sophia looked across at him with pride gleaming in her eyes.

'Gretton Tur, the mighty one will be avenged,' she yelled to mounting cheers.

'Follow us now!' her husband continued.

As Piotre Andresen spoke the final words he raised the black staff high over his head. There was a groaning, rumbling sound that built up quickly to a deafening

CRACK! Suddenly, a huge swirling hole seemed to open up in front of the Andresens and their black holva. It was bigger than any pathway that Jacques had ever seen and made his mouth gape open in wonder and admiration at what his father had done.

'My son,' his father was shouting at him over the noise of the rish, 'ride with me now to glory and victory.'

Spurring the holva on, father, mother and son disappeared into the swirling light of the pathway, followed closely by the slavering mass of rish.

Tarawen cowered back in his hiding place, riven with fear at what he had just witnessed. In all his experience he had never seen such an army.

He waited until all of the rish and holva had finally disappeared through the pathway. With a blinding flash of red light it vanished, leaving swirling eddies of dust in the air. Then he scrambled to his feet and began running back to where he had tethered his horse in the shelter of the nearby trees.

He had to get back to the rebel camp. He had to get a message to Vishan on Beltheron.

Interference

'Both of you must stay here indoors,' Jenn said to Helen and Serrion. 'The birds are gathering right overhead. It's like a black cloud of the horrible creatures.'

She was right. The numbers of birds had been growing all morning. They flew overhead in huge flocks; they perched together on rooftops, fences, trees and towers; they cawed and screeched to each other continuously in a raucous clamour.

During the night many more had flown into the windows – whether by accident or design no one knew – and Matt had been securing heavy wooden panels onto the inside of the window frames. The room downstairs where they had all gathered was lit by candles that threw threatening flickers against the walls. Everyone was extremely tense.

Jenn had tried to contact people through the silverscreen, but all she managed to pick up was a grainy snowstorm of static and buzzing noise. She switched it off in frustration.

Just as the silverscreen faded, Jenn thought she saw the outline of a familiar face staring out at her for a moment. 'No, it couldn't be,' she thought to herself and thought no more about it.

'I wish we knew what was going on out there,' Matt said for the tenth time that morning.

'What's wrong with the silverscreen?' Helen asked.

'I'm not sure, but it seems to have been blocked in some way,' her mother replied.

Suddenly there was a loud hammering at the door. They all jumped.

'It's them! The birds! The birds are trying to get in!' Helen yelled in panic.

Her father placed his hand on her shoulder. 'I don't think so,' he reassured them. 'This sounds different to me.'

The hammering was repeated – even more urgently than before. Matt ran over to the door.

'Stand back, just in case,' he warned them.

Matt turned the heavy brass key in the old lock and cautiously opened the door a fraction.

'About time!' came a familiar voice. 'Now please let me in before I am pecked to tatters!'

Matt threw the door wide with a relieved grin and Cleve Harrow stepped into the room. He slammed it closed again immediately. There were several birds already turning in the air to swoop down.

'Cleve! Thank goodness!'

'Are you alright!'

'What's happening out there?'

'What's making the birds do this?'

Cleve Harrow silenced their questions with a wave of his hand. Then they saw the expression on his face. It shocked all four of them. They had never seen the Cleve look so anguished.

'Terrible things are happening,' he began. 'There is dreadful danger here in the city for all of us now.'

He moved across to Serrion. Harrow swallowed hard a couple of times and then continued.

'I am sorry, my boy, but I have the most awful news for you. Sit down.'

Serrion did so. An overwhelming feeling of dread swept over him.

Slowly, painfully, Harrow told Serrion what had happened to Korellia.

Behind them, Matt gave a grunt of anger, Jenn gasped and Helen began to weep softly. But Serrion himself showed no reaction. He sat perfectly still, gazing at a blank space on the wall opposite as he listened to the Cleve's words.

Eventually Serrion spoke. Just two words.

'My mother.'

There was complete silence in the room. No one moved. Then Serrion continued.

'Two years. I had just two years with her. First they leave and take everything I ever knew or believed with them. Then they take *her* from me.'

Serrion took a great, gasping breath. 'Poor Mum. Poor Mum.'

Now it seemed as if the tears might finally come, as if the huge grief that he felt would take over. But instead Serrion breathed out sharply in an expression of disbelief and disgust. 'Why do they hate me so much?' The tears were blinked back and his eyes were cold and hard once more.

There was another long silence. Then Serrion seemed to shake himself and he looked up at Harrow.

'Orianna,' he said quickly, 'does Orianna know?'

Harrow nodded briefly. 'She has been told.'

'Is she alright?' Serrion continued. 'I should be with her. Where is she?

'Parenon is looking after her. She will be safe. I have sent them away from the city.'

Serrion nodded. 'That's good. Thank you, Cleve.'

Serrion's voice sounded very different all of a sudden. It was much more serious and mature.

'Thank you my friend, for looking after my sister,' he continued. 'She will be safest and best comforted with Parenon right now.'

Then he continued staring at the wall.

The Meeting

Piotre and Sophia Andresen and their son Jacques arrived in the land of Beltheron under cover of a heavy black cloud. They were on high ground at the edge of a bare plain some three miles from Beltheron City itself.

The huge pathway that had opened up for them was still depositing a large number of rish, holva and weaponry all around them on the gently sloping hill. You could see the bare, drab plain of Atros behind them through the opening. It was, quite literally, a window onto another world.

Soon the army was complete and the shimmering circular hole of the pathway closed with a wailing sound like the scream of a young child.

The rish began to make camp. They tethered their scaly steeds to trees and began to build fires to cook their vile-smelling meat.

The brannoch creature, Jacques' new 'pet' had also traveled through the pathway with them. Now it had been chained up, with four rish to guard it. It strained against the heavy metal chains. The guards edged away from the beast as it snarled under its breath at them.

Once these preparations had been achieved, the three Andresens rode their dark holva away from the camp to the brow of a nearby hill. It was still some distance from the city itself.

Deep crimson streaks ran across the horizon, and

higher up the sky was a clear, deep blue.

A large, black shape flew out of the fading light of late afternoon. It was a massive raven. Its ragged wings flapped as it came to land at their feet. The huge bird stood with its head cocked to one side; evil, glinting eyes regarded them with amusement. Larena.

'Noble Lord,' Larena spoke in her harsh, cawing bird's voice.

'My trusted friend,' Piotre Andresen replied, bowing his head slightly to the birdwoman.

Sophia dismounted from her holva and walked over to their old accomplice. She stood close to Larena and began to stroke the black head of the bird gently.

'All is going perfectly to plan,' Larena continued. 'My flocks are gathering on rooftops and trees throughout that stinking city.'

She flapped one wing contemptuously in the direction of Beltheron in the distance.

'I am delighted to offer you all the assistance you need to overrun this place.'

'Wonderful!' Sophia replied. 'Thank you, my old friend. We couldn't have wished for a better diversion for our attack. Everything is working out just as we wished.'

Piotre sneered. 'This place has been lazy and self-satisfied for too long,' he said. 'It will be a delight to finally take control and tell old Ungolin face to face what I really think of him.'

'And when we do Father,' Jacques replied in a breathless voice, 'when we do, we will turn their sorry little lives upside down. I want to make them squirm with fear and pain.'

Both his parents grinned proudly at him.

'Most of all I want to make sure that brat Serrion gets what's coming to him.' His words were now little more than a snarl. 'He humiliated me two years ago – left me for dead in the Wild Lord's castle. Well now it's my turn for revenge.'

'Patience my son,' Sophia said. She moved away from Larena and back to the chomping, foamy mouth of her son's holva. Grabbing the reins she pulled the head of the steed to one side so she could look directly up into her Jacques' face.

'It will happen soon, my boy. Very soon.'

Her words seemed to calm him immediately. As he looked down at her he smiled. It did not soften his hard face though, and his eyes remained cold.

'It will happen immediately,' Piotre announced.

'Yes, right now,' Sophia replied. 'And it will bring about the darkest day in Beltheron's history.'

'I must fly back to the city,' Larena's croaking voice cut through the gloom of the evening. 'I will prepare my birds for any help they may give you and meet with you again at the sight of our victory!'

Larena spread her wings and took off into the darkening sky. As she flew higher, several more crows flew out of the trees, wheeled around in the sky and joined Larena as she flew towards Beltheron City.

It seemed to be late in the evening even though a glance at the time tower would have shown that it was still only the end of the afternoon. Even so the streets of Beltheron City were all practically deserted. No one dared to venture out beyond their own doorstep. Dark drapes hung in most of the windows.

Even in one of the main market squares of Beltheron, by the time tower itself, only a handful of people remained. Here, large crowds would ordinarily be gathered, bartering, laughing and chattering. It seemed unnatural that there should be so few in such a vast space. Those that were there now all hurried across the square as quickly as they could, or clung to the shadows of the walls to avoid the eyes of the birds that wheeled overhead.

Suddenly, stones began to fall from the buildings around the market square. The time tower shook to its very foundations and a groaning grinding sound – like that of some immense machine – rent the air.

The citizens of Beltheron City peered through their windows to look at this new horror and clutched their ears at the sound. They scurried for shelter under tables and beds, in cupboards, anywhere to get away from that terrible noise.

But what shelter could there be when the ground itself began to quake and shudder?

Then, with a low *whump!* sound that reverberated through the whole body, the air in the middle of the market square distorted. A hole over ten metres in diameter opened up. Looking at this hole was like looking through the frosted glass on a bathroom window into a swirl of smoke and livid flame.

Swiftly the image began to clear. Twisted shapes started to take on a more solid form and a strange landscape could be seen through the opening. There were fields and bare, black-limbed trees with dark jagged mountains rising behind. It was like looking the wrong way round through a telescope at some distant land.

In the next moment there came a neighing, whinnying sound. A group of holva leapt through the opening and onto the cobbled stones of Beltheron's market square.

The rider of the first holva held a black staff triumphantly above his head. He was a tall agile man with a hard, angular face and piercing blue eyes. Piotre

Andresen, servant of Gretton Tur, galloped into the middle of Beltheron City with his wife and son at his side. Hordes of rish, holva and other Atrossian men poured through the entrance after them.

Together they all rode triumphantly through the market square. The opening of the pathway closed up behind the last figures to stagger through. (It happened to be Crudpile and Dross who, as usual, were doing their best to keep themselves out of the thick of the danger.)

The brannoch did its job of keeping the pulver at bay. Even held on chains by the rish it snarled so fiercely that the soldiers stayed back. It ran up to the length of its metal leashes to snap at all who did have the courage to come near. Just as Piotre had imagined, the creature instilled terror and weakened their enemy so that they did not dare to mount a full attack.

And so, unthreatened, they all rode down wide avenues – the Andresen's fearsome army – directly to Ungolin's palace and the great hall.

Soon the towers of the palace rose up above them out of the darkness and through the thick clouds to unseen heights. Word of the brannoch might have gone on ahead of them, for no guards met them as they proceeded up the steps to the huge doors.

Piotre swung a long black staff out from under his cloak and pointed it at the doors. With a shuddering crack the ancient wood was torn asunder No pulver challenged them. Sophia was right; Larena and her battalions of birds had provided them with the perfect diversion. The pulver were scattered throughout the corridors and rooms, fighting off flocks of starlings and rooks that had flown inside.

And so - completely unchallenged - the Beltheron Select walked into the heart of Ungolin's domain.

Warning Light

On the other side of the city, Harrow was still in the downstairs room with Matt, Jenn, Helen and Serrion. They had been talking to Serrion and trying their best to comfort him. He had said very little for the last half hour or so. Helen sat next to him holding one of his hands in both of hers, gently stroking the back of it with her fingers.

Jenn had brewed a calming drink from some of the pungent herbs in one of her large earthenware bottles in the kitchen. She told him that it would help him to relax if he drank it while it was still hot and steaming, but he had hardly touched it. The mug remained on the low table in front of him. The others all looked around at each other, sorrow and concern etched on their faces.

Suddenly Serrion froze. A searing red light flashed before his eyes. It was like one of his premonitions, but this had no rhyme or reason. It didn't seem to come from anywhere. There was no reflection from another object; the light hadn't any point of reference in the room at all. It had simply appeared, suddenly filling his vision.

'Helen…Harrow…Something's happening. There's something dreadfully wrong.'

'Boy?' Harrow began to stand and move slowly towards him.

'What is it?' asked Jenn. She was already up on her feet, a worried expression on her face. She was across the room in a moment, holding onto Serrion's shoulders and gazing intently into his face.

Serrion blinked a couple of times to try to clear his vision. He was aware of Helen's comforting hands on his own and he could sense Harrow's presence nearby, but it was almost as if he had been blinded by the red light.

In a flash his vision cleared. But he was not looking at the room. He could not see Helen, Matt, Jenn or the Cleve any more. Instead he was looking directly into Lord Ungolin's great hall.

All of a sudden the face of Ungolin himself filled Serrion's vision. The old man was screaming. Serrion gave a cry of shock and Helen's fingers tightened around his hand, digging into the palm.

'Serrion! Serrion! Tell me, please! What is it? What's wrong?'

Harrow was now intoning soothing words softly into his ear. Serrion felt their magical calming effect immediately and began to speak. His words came slowly and thickly.

'The great hall. Ungolin's in danger. We must get to him!'

Piotre, Sophia and Jacques Andresen moved through the building swiftly. Each guard they encountered in the corridors was dispatched without a thought or a backward glance by a quick flick of the black staff held in Piotre's hands. None of the pulver could withstand the blast of such a terrible weapon and all crumpled to the ground.

They approached a wide staircase with intricate tapestries and paintings hanging on the walls. At the top of the staircase was a huge set of oak doors. Once more Piotre raised the staff and blasted a hole through the centre of it. When the smoke cleared the wood lay splintered into pieces on the ground and hanging from the twisted hinges.

Father and son sped up the last few steps and leapt over the broken threshold. Sophia remained at the bottom of the staircase for a few moments. She looked around one final time to make sure no more foolhardy guards were following them. She then hurried up the steps after the others.

Now they were only a few short paces away from Ungolin's hall. Piotre took a small black ball from one of the pockets of his cloak and threw it down behind him. A shimmering wall appeared from floor to ceiling where the oak door had been, shutting them off completely from the outside.

'That will stop anyone from interfering with us,' he said. Sophia and Jacques smiled back at him.

'Now we are safely inside,' Sophia said to Piotre. 'I will prepare a pathway to bring our creature in to join us.'

'One of these anterooms should be perfect,' he replied, gesturing to one of the smaller rooms off to one side of the passage.

Sophia nodded and disappeared through the doorway. Piotre and Jacques began to move towards the great hall.

A final solitary guard had remained on duty by the door. Now he ran out and stood in their way. He held a long sword in front of him.

'Halt or I will…'

He spoke no more as a blast from Jacques' outstretched hand hit him square in the chest and knocked him against the opposite wall.

'Or you will do what, fool?' Jacques grinned.

Piotre and his son jumped over the inert body of the guard, into the hall itself and ran straight towards Ungolin's huge chair on its raised platform.

Ungolin had been sitting on his throne on the raised

dais, with one of his advisors, deep in consultation over a bundle of papers. They had heard all the commotion outside and both had spun around in surprise so that now they were facing the entrance as the Andresens entered.

'What is the meaning of this outrage!' the old advisor began to cry out.

'Silence!' Piotre fired a blast from the black staff and the poor man fell to the ground in a crumpled heap.

Ungolin was now on his feet. He seemed tall on the raised dais of the throne, and although his body was old and withered, his voice was firm and rang out clearly as he spoke.

'At last you dare to come to me and show your treacherous, unholy face,' he said to Piotre.

'You ancient fool! You still think your words hold power,' his enemy replied. 'Yet in reality you have no power left at all. Your advisors are dead or fleeing, your soldiers fall like leaves on a winter tree and your most trusted alliances have withered to nothing.'

Ungolin managed a bitter laugh.

'You don't ever change, do you Andresen?' he said. 'Even now you cannot resist coming here to gloat.'

'If you think that is the only reason for my return to Beltheron, then your wits are even more addled than I had dared to hope for.'

'Then why *are* you here?' Ungolin answered. 'You know that in spite of your boasts, your return here can only bring about your own death and ruin.' He turned towards Jacques. 'I had heard that you were dead already,' he hissed at the young man. 'Unfortunately I was mistaken. Never mind, hopefully we can soon rectify that error.' His gaze intensified until it made Jacques flinch backwards in fear.

His father, however, was not so easily cowered by the ancient power in Ungolin's words and manner.

'Your threats are worthless. We have come to take control,' he said simply. 'To place ourselves on your throne, and rule Beltheron.'

'Ha! That will never be,' Ungolin replied.

'You will tell me all that I ask,' Piotre continued.

'Never!'

'There are details I need to know; passwords, the location of certain sets of keys etc.'

'I will never surrender my knowledge to you!'

Piotre merely smiled wider at Ungolin's defiance.

'Most importantly of all, you will tell me where I can lay my hands on the golden staff.'

Ungolin stiffened even more.

'You will tell me willingly, old man, or it will be the worse for you.'

'You can kill me in a hundred ways and I will never divulge any of my city's secrets,' Ungolin sputtered through clenched teeth. 'Certainly not about the golden staff.'

'I *will* kill you, old fool, and it will feel like a *thousand* deaths, not a hundred!'

As he said this, Piotre twisted his hand and Ungolin suddenly clutched at his heart. The brave old warrior tried to stifle the pain, using his own strong magics to dull the shock. Even so he could not stop himself crying out in agony at the stabbing fingers of fire that seemed to clutch at his lungs and heart. He could not breathe.

Piotre's thin fingers twitched above Ungolin's head and a dribble of red blood trickled from the corner of the old Lord's mouth. Each attempt to breathe brought further panic as Ungolin fought to get air and realised he was drowning in his own blood.

'Tell me!' Piotre hissed. 'Tell me and I will end this quickly!'

Jacques grinned malevolently as he watched his father

twist his hand once more and heard Ungolin gasp with the last of his breath.

'Do it Father!' he yelled. 'Do it!'

'Where is the golden staff?'

Suddenly there was a flash behind them, followed by the sound of running footsteps and then another voice in the room.

'Leave him you Hell Fiend!'

The voice came from the shattered entranceway behind them. The shimmering force field that Piotre Andresen had created by the oak door had gone. Piotre continued to concentrate on Ungolin, not troubled by this sudden intrusion, but Jacques spun around, impatient anger on his face.

There stood Cleve Harrow. Serrion was directly behind him. He was shaking his hands and flexing his fingers after the effort of opening up the Andresen's protective barrier on the door.

Serrion saw Jacques and Piotre standing there and it seemed as if the stone floor had tilted under his feet. There was his sworn enemy, Jacques, still alive after all!

But even more shocking and disturbing than that, standing in front of him was the man whom he had called 'Dad' for the first twelve years of his life. Serrion's eyes began to prickle as sadness, regret and deep rage flowed through him. His legs almost buckled beneath him.

Serrion now saw everything through a thick, red light. It flooded his vision. This red light that usually warned him of danger now appeared to be fueled by his own sorrow and rage. And it was growing stronger all the time.

Harrow stepped further into the chamber. The golden staff of Beltheron was clutched tightly in his hands. Ungolin's face fell as he saw it.

'Oh no! Cleve, you should not have come here,' he

began. 'You should not have brought...'

Jacques grinned.

'It's working, father,' he said with exultation. 'He brought it right to us, just like you said he would!'

Piotre instantly released his grip on Ungolin and spun towards Harrow. In one quick, fluid movement he brought up the black staff with his right hand, and threw a ball of yellow fire at the Cleve's head with the other. It clung to his head like an angry swarm of bees. At the same moment, Jacques thrust his own hands forwards, flinging the Cleve off balance.

Serrion lifted his palm instinctively and, without understanding how, he parried the blow from Jacques before it could do any further damage. He sent the jet of energy up to the furthest corner of the room where it sputtered out harmlessly in a shower of tiny sparks. Was his gift of opening locks by moving objects somehow growing stronger through the anger he felt? Harrow had begun to intone a strange incantation and the swarm of yellow fire around his head grew dim.

'Cleve, are you alright?'

Harrow nodded. 'My magic – what I have of it – is still strong enough to break the trickery of this churl.'

Serrion spun round towards his enemies. The red light through which he was seeing everything around him started to dim, but it had left him with a surging energy that tingled in his hands. He felt it pulse up his arms. It made him feel terribly powerful.

He was about to draw the sword from his belt when he heard a low, rattling growl behind him. He turned swiftly.

The sight that met his eyes made him turn cold with horror.

Standing in the doorway was Jacques' new "pet", that foul creature, the brannoch. It had a human form, but the texture of its skin was slick, wet and smooth like grey metal. Muscles rippled under the surface and the creature twitched continuously, as if there were insects, repeatedly stinging or nibbling away. This horrible being began to move towards him, slowly and purposefully, its sharp teeth bared in expectant delight.

Sophia stood in the doorway behind the beast. 'Oh good,' she said as she saw Serrion. 'I see we got here just in time for the reunion.'

Serrion staggered again at the sight of Sophia.

Piotre and Jacques were still grinning triumphantly. The grey, slimy creature began to lick its lips. Its tongue worked around its sharp fangs.

'Harrow, what do I do?' Serrion called. His voice rose higher in panic.

'There is nothing you can do, my boy.' Harrow sounded totally defeated. 'It is a brannoch. The only thing to do is… RUN!'

His voice suddenly rang clear throughout the hall. At the same time, Harrow flung an explosion of yellow energy in front of the creature in an attempt to distract it. However, Piotre flicked his hand and the flare fizzled out in a wisp of smoke. The brannoch didn't even blink.

Serrion didn't need to be told to run twice. Leaping back across the great hall, he plunged through the doorway, the strength that he had felt a moment before making him move faster than normal.

Jacques unfurled a piece of white cloth from his pocket and waved it under the brannoch's nose. It sniffed at the scrap of Serrion's old shirt hungrily. Slobber dripped from its jaws. A snickering whine escaped its throat, like a dog waiting patiently to be fed.

'Your time has come, my pet,' Jacques said. 'Now… FETCH!'

Pastoral

Orianna and Parenon were sitting together in the hollowed out trunk of an ancient oak tree. It was the evening of the same day they had been sent away from the city by Cleve Harrow.

The hollow tree opened onto an entrance to a network of tunnels and rooms that led deep into the side of a hill in the middle of a forest. These tunnels and rooms were originally created to be used as a hiding place and emergency meeting rooms for Ungolin and his close advisors in times of emergency. More recently it had been occupied by a handful of pulver captains and guards during training exercises in the forest.

The place was still a closely guarded secret however, and apart from Cleve Harrow, Ungolin and those few pulver captains, no one knew of its exact location. Parenon had been there before though, and he recognized the place as soon as the pathway had dropped them there.

Orianna was in bad shape, he knew. She had not spoken since they had arrived, and was now rocking herself backwards and forwards. It seemed as if the full shock of the news about her mother had finally hit her.

He felt quite helpless. Even at the best of times he had always found it difficult to know what to say to Orianna. Every time she came into a room he felt tongue-tied and knew that his cheeks were growing bright red with embarrassment. But now it was as if someone had stolen his voice away completely. He knew how to protect her from danger and he would lay down his life to save her from the violence of battle, but he had no idea at all how to deal with *this* situation. What could he say to comfort her?

'Stay here,' he whispered to her. 'I will get us something to eat.'

He wandered off a little way through the trees. His pulver training made him aware of any sound or the slightest trail of a creature on the forest floor. He checked behind him continually, keeping Orianna in sight while he hunted for food. He knew he should have taken her down into the tunnels, but she shook her head at that suggestion when they arrived. It was dark and dismal down there, he had to admit. She seemed more comfortable out under the open skies in the fresh air.

He didn't have to go far before he spied a small, furry creature with a long body and short, stubby legs. 'A steasle,' he thought. 'Not much meat on them, but very tasty.' He reached for his hunting knife.

Soon they were cooking over a small campfire. It crackled and hissed in the shallow dip that Parenon had scooped out in the soft earth. He had then piled the earth to one side so that he could use it to put out the light and smother the tell-tale smoke instantly should they need to.

So far however, they had been undisturbed.

The smells from the cooking steasle were a comfort to Orianna, even in her distracted state, and at last she began to speak to Parenon as he prepared the meat over the flames.

'Mother always supported my decision when I said I wanted to go to study with Harrow,' she said.

Parenon didn't reply, but just nodded encouragement.

He knew that it would be helpful for Orianna to talk about Korellia, and he was prepared to listen.

'She knew how important it was for me, and she never stood in my way. Even when it would have been easier for her if I had stayed at home to help her.' Orianna was still gazing into the crackling fire. She spoke slowly and softly, lost in her memories.

'And Mother was right, it *was* good for me,' she continued. 'It was something I was fascinated by and I spent hours and hours studying with the Cleve.'

Orianna paused for a moment. She looked up into the overarching branches of the tree, deep in thought. Then she grinned at herself.

'I was never very comfortable around boys,' she continued, 'and most of them thought I was a bit boring anyway, just interested in my books and old knowledge all the time.'

'*I* never thought that you were boring,' Parenon said, and then immediately wished he hadn't. Orianna looked away from the surrounding trees and straight into his eyes (he had been staring at her all the time she had been speaking). He turned away. What had he been thinking? Why had he said that? She would think he was an idiot!

Orianna smiled. He was so sweet when he blushed! What was it her mother had called him? 'Your Parenon.' In that moment it seemed that Korellia was giving her blessing to her daughter. A wave of relief washed through Orianna. In spite of all the tragedy and fear surrounding them, maybe one thing might turn out to the good for them both.

'Thank you for saying that,' she whispered. 'And you were the one boy that I *did* feel comfortable with.'

Parenon's complexion turned to a deep beetroot

colour. His heart was pounding as hard as if he were facing a horde of rish soldiers. He swallowed hard.

'Orianna,' he began, 'I think… I think…'

'Yes, Parenon,' Orianna breathed. 'What is it you want to say?'

'I think … I think that…'

'Yes?'

'Orianna, I think the steasle is burning.'

There was a moment's silence then both of them erupted into gales of laughter. The happy sound, the first that had been heard on Beltheron throughout that long day, echoed up into the trees and across the forest.

Hunt of the Brannoch

It felt as if a hundred memories were spinning around in Serrion's head as he ran. Dozens of mundane everyday moments while he had been growing up: his mother lifting him up to the window to look at a rainbow when he was only four years old; his father in his chair at home, absorbed in his papers but looking up to help him with his homework; holding onto both their hands to swing between them when they were all out walking together. All these images were now bitterly twisted in Serrion's head, ruined forever.

He had gradually come to terms with the lies and betrayals over the last couple of years, but coming face to face with Piotre and Sophia again had brought all of the pain surging back. Not his mother! Not his father! They were the enemy. They had caused the death of hie real mother and were now trying to kill him! He had to banish those other memories of them forever!

He had sped out of the great hall without once looking back. He could still hear Harrow's voice calling behind him, urging him to run.

The brannoch could not be far behind him. He could hear its scaly feet rasping against the flagstones on the floor of the corridor. Serrion was almost at a doorway. He hurled himself through it swinging his hand behind him as he did so to slam the door locked behind him. He hoped that would delay the creature long enough for him to escape.

Outside in the piazza his chances didn't improve much. The Atrossian forces were setting up camp in front of Ungolin's palace. They had tied their holva up to feed from water troughs and sacks of grain and were erecting tents all around him. He sank back into the shadows of the doorway. His breath was already ragged with panic.

Which way could he go? He could hear the scrabbling of the brannoch behind the door. Serrion didn't know exactly how strong the creature was, but he had been convinced by Harrow's look of fear when he had first seen the creature and knew that a mere door wouldn't stop it for long.

As he watched the rish in the piazza it seemed that – just for a moment – luck was on his side. With a loud cry of 'for Mage and Council!' a group of pulver ran out from an alleyway at the opposite side of the piazza. They were brandishing swords and spears. The attention of the rish was drawn away from the palace entrance as a number of them lurched angrily towards the pulver.

Spears flew, a few rish fell, but it was only a quick skirmish. In under a minute the rish beat them back and the pulver had to retreat again to shelter, but it had been long enough for Serrion. By the time the rish had recovered from the surprise attack, he had sped away from the palace doorway and was running through the shadows to a side alley.

As he ran he looked into every doorway. He could have opened any one of the doors and stepped inside of course, but he did not want to bring danger to any of the families who lived there. No, he realised, he had to choose his hiding place more carefully.

The alley finally opened out into a wider street. It was completely deserted here, he was pleased to see. All of the rish forces must be concentrated into the main piazza behind him. He paused for a moment and for the first time since he had started running, he looked behind him. There was still nothing following him. Perhaps he had been lucky! Perhaps the brannoch had lost the scent of him already! Hope surged up inside his heart. The battle was not over. All was not forsaken. He still had a chance to find safety, and to make those guilty of Korellia's death pay the price.

But even as thoughts of revenge began to take hold, he saw the brannoch race around the corner at the opposite end of the alley and come charging towards him.

He glanced up and down the street. To his left there was just a long open road, with no chance of a hiding place. Fifty metres or so to his right however, was a tall building. It looked like a large warehouse, but there was a high bell tower at one end. The building had several floors rising up from street level and an idea began to form in Serrion's mind. The building looked deserted. He raced towards it.

He could hear the brannoch gaining on him. In sheer panic he looked behind him. The creature was already out of the alleyway and hurtling towards him. With a sickening lurch in his stomach Serrion saw that even though the brannoch was shaped roughly like a human, it had dropped down onto all fours and was now running like a dog – as fast as a greyhound.

Plunging through the door he swung it closed behind him. Serrion slid the heavy metal bolt closed with an easy flick of his hand. Metal bolts were not enough to stop this pursuer though. With a groaning cracking sound the door buckled inwards as the brannoch hit it from outside.

Serrion didn't hesitate. He turned away from the door and hurried towards a nearby staircase. As soon as he had looked across the street and seen this high building, an image had come into his head. Whether it was another premonition, or just a wild, crazy last idea of escape he couldn't tell. He just knew the only chance to get away from the brannoch was to climb, to get higher.

He reached the base of the stairwell and started to climb the steps just as he heard the brannoch break through the door. It scrambled through the twisted, splintered shards. It pushed them aside with its immensely strong arms as if they were made of cardboard.

Serrion sped upwards. He had to get higher.

The stairs wound in a wide spiral around a central stone column. They were flat and broad, so there was little chance of him losing his footing. He raced upwards as fast as his tired legs would carry him, ignoring the aches that screamed at him from his exhausted muscles.

The brannoch had spotted him and with a fevered howl it ran towards him. It was now back on its legs again and running like a man, pumping its arms to gain momentum. Spittle flew from its jaws as it closed on the base of the stairs.

It was lucky that Serrion had a head start, for while he was struggling up one step at a time the brannoch was leaping upwards, missing two or three stairs with each pace. He was gaining at a frightening rate.

Up and up they went, until at last he had a stroke of good fortune. Serrion came to a heavy metal gate that was closed across the stairwell. It had been placed there as a security measure so that only authorised officials working there could get to the very top. It did not stop Serrion of course. Out shot his hand and the metal swung open. Through the gate he raced, with the brannoch lurching ever closer. Serrion flung his arm wide behind him, his fingers splayed open. He clenched his fist and the metal swung closed again, locking tightly.

The creature hit the gate at a terrific pace. The gate buckled under the pressure but held firm.

Serrion didn't waste a moment. He knew that the brannoch could break through. He turned and ran on upwards.

At last he reached the top of the stairs. It opened out onto a platform. He was at the top of the bell tower that he had seen from the street below. There was a huge bell hanging there and below it an open shaft down which hung the rope that was used to ring it from the ground floor. He realised that the spiral staircase he had just climbed had actually wound around this central shaft.

A number of thin stone columns supported the domed roof of the bell tower around the edge of the platform. Serrion walked across to them. He held onto one of the columns to lean out and peer over the edge. The tower dropped away below him without a ledge or any handholds to help him. He could not escape that way. He turned around again and looked down the central shaft of the bell tower itself.

He could see that the rope winding away down the middle of the shaft was a thick one. Easily thick enough to hold his weight, he thought. He reached out over the gaping fall of the shaft and managed to grasp hold of the rope. Serrion pulled it towards him. All the time he could hear the growling and snarling of the brannoch, only a handful of steps below him. There was also a rhythmic thumping sound as the brannoch struck the gate again and again in fury.

Serrion pulled the rope taut. Would it take his weight? The pulley above looked sturdy. His heart was hammering in his chest and his mouth had turned dry and sticky with fear. He could not even see the bottom of the shaft. It faded away into darkness below him.

Suddenly he heard the sound that he had feared. With a creaking, groan and a clang the gates below were shattered by the strength and ferocity of the brannoch. He heard it give a yowl of triumph as it began to scramble up towards him once more.

Serrion still had the rope in his hands. He hesitated. Should he climb down? An image rose up in his head of the brannoch slicing through the rope above him, leaving him to tumble into the darkness to his death.

In another moment the decision was taken from him as the brannoch rounded the last bend up onto the platform and plunged into him. The impact drove the air from Serrion's lungs. Snarling ferociously the brannoch snapped at his head as they tumbled backwards. Serrion just had time to wrap his hand more firmly around the rope before they were both tipped over the edge and fell into the shaft of the bell tower.

As the rope was pulled down with their weight, the bell above began to peel with a deafening sound. The rope jerked taut and Serrion felt his shoulders wrenched as he was brought up sharply. The brannoch's grip on Serrion was torn away with the jolt and it began to fall further down the shaft. Serrion grunted with the effort of maintaining his own hold on the rope above.

Before it could fall too far the brannoch caught onto a large stone that stuck out of one side of the wall. It held on grimly about five metres below him. With its other arm the brannoch lashed out and took the rope in its claws. The creature was now wrestling with the rope, pulling it sharply this way and that trying to shake Serrion off. The bell rang out madly above them as it did so.

Serrion tried to swing himself across to the side so that he could take hold of the edge of the bell tower and climb over onto the platform again, but at the same time his pursuer below jumped onto the rope itself. The full weight of the brannoch was too much for the pulley above the bell and the wood gave way. Serrion, brannoch, rope and bell lurched downwards into the shaft. They were brought up sharply after dropping just a metre or so as the wood of the pulley held firm once more as it wedged against the wall of the shaft. But now the bell had dropped down into the shaft itself, below the level of the platform.

Serrion glanced down. The creature was beginning to struggle upwards towards him.

There was nothing for it now, Serrion thought grimly. He would have to climb up or he was dead.

Across the city, in the great hall, Piotre and Cleve Harrow were still locked in battle over the golden staff. Flares of light crackled around the room between them, fired with fury from the end of both the black and golden staffs in their hands. Such was their intense rage that neither Sophia nor Jacques felt they could intervene.

Sophia heard the sound of a distant bell ringing out across the city. Curious to what it might be she rushed to the door and called out into the passageway outside.

'Larena!'

The Birdwoman came flying in.

'Mistress?'

'Someone is ringing a bell from one of the towers. We cannot take any chances. It could be a pulver trying to send a message, or a warning to others. See to it.'

'Of course, mistress,' Larena replied. 'I will send a couple of my hawks to investigate.'

She flapped her wings and flew from the building.

Meanwhile, Piotre had used this distraction to gain the upper hand over Harrow. With a lurch of his hand, a lightning bolt shot towards the Cleve, knocking him off balance. The golden staff sped through the air towards Jacques' waiting grasp.

'Thanks Father!' he yelled as his fingers closed over the long awaited prize.

Harrow realised there was nothing now he could do. Ungolin lay in a still, crumpled heap on the floor. With a deep breath, he drew his robes around him and uttered a low incantation. In a flash of light he was gone before any of the Andresen family could do anything to stop him.

The harsh rope was beginning to burn Serrion's fingers and palms. Bit by bit he crawled up, hand over hand. The brannoch was gaining on him. It was able to get a firmer grip with its feet, and its strength was far greater than Serrion's.

He had never felt so terrified. He gripped with his knees as tightly as he could and used the very last of his strength to haul himself a little higher. He knew that he was only postponing the horrible, inevitable moment when the brannoch finally caught up with him. Why had he come up here? What insane thought was it that had told him he had to climb to a high place? His foresight had not let him down before and yet he now knew he would have been far better off just running and hiding.

Just then he felt the creature's hot breath on his ankles. He considered letting go of the rope and simply falling away into oblivion. But then there was a battering of wings above him. He looked up and saw two large hawks coming in to land between the pillars on the platform of the bell tower. They began to caw and screech excitedly as they caught sight of him.

He looked up into the inside of the large bell itself.

The combined weight on the rope of both Serrion and the brannoch had pulled the bell so far over to one side that it was now lodged against the bricks on the inside of the shaft wall. The round metal clapper of the bell hung down on a leather strap. With a grunt of energy he pulled himself upwards once more. Another idea came to him. He was now level with the inside of the dome of the bell. He realised it was big enough for him to climb up inside it. If he could only reach out and grab hold of the clapper then he might be able to…

Too late! In that moment the brannoch grabbed his foot. Serrion screamed in shock and pain. Its claws had cut into his ankle. The sound of his cry excited the birds even more. They flew down into the shaft of the bell tower pecking and cawing at the two figures struggling on the swaying rope.

The brannoch became even more furious at the arrival of the birds. It let go of Serrion's ankle and swung around wildly to grab at these new, feathered attackers.

As the brannoch lurched around it caused the rope to swing in closer towards the bell. Serrion took his chance. He let go with one hand and grabbed the clapper. The metal was smooth and slippery but it was his only chance. Taking a deep breath he let go of the rope with the other hand and swung out under the tilted dome of the bell. His fingers held firm on the rounded ball of metal. He clutched desperately to get a purchase on the leather strap of the clapper with his other hand as the birds flapped only centimeters from his face.

Luckily they were still more concerned with the brannoch. In that moment, the hawks did not know, or care, that this creature was a servant of their allies. Their instincts only told them that here was a dangerous predator, a threat to bird-kind.

The narrow confines of the shaft made it difficult for any of them, bird or brannoch, to gain the upper hand in the struggle. They swooped at its snarling face with their talons slashing. This kept the creature occupied and gave Serrion a few extra moments. At last his fingers managed to get hold of the strap and he pulled himself up inside the dome of the great bell.

After climbing hand over hand a few more times he found that he could bring up one leg and balance his foot on the clapper. The angle of the bell made it possible to rest his other foot on the inside of the bell itself. This immediately took some of the pressure off the muscles in his arms, which were now screaming in agony.

When he felt his balance was secure he risked a look down.

The brannoch was still lurching wildly on the rope directly underneath him, its snarls and rapid angry movements only aggravating the hawks more and more.

Then, with one final flailing movement towards the hawks, the brannoch lost its grip on the rope. It began to fall – slowly at first, as it seemed to Serrion – and with a terrible howl it tumbled away into the darkness below. It bounced off the sides of the tower twice before disappearing completely from view.

As the brannoch's weight was released from the rope, the bell swung back away from the wall. It continued its pendulum movement backwards and forwards so that Serrion found himself being battered against one side then the other – like a human clapper – as he hung on.

He was vaguely aware of a crunching thud from far, far below as the brannoch hit the ground at the bottom of the shaft.

The two hawks seemed to have forgotten Serrion in his hiding place inside the bell. They flew back up outside and were soon swooping back towards the great hall.

Serrion clung on until the bell had stopped swinging. Both feet rested on the top of the clapper. He rested inside the dome of the bell for a while until he could feel some strength returning to his arms and legs.

'This next bit could be tricky,' he thought, as he considered how he was going to get down.

The rope was hanging to one side of the bell. It was too far away for him to reach, and he daren't take a leap and just hope to grab it. He rested on the clapper for a few more moments, thinking hard.

Finally he made a decision. Lowering himself until he was sitting on the clapper with his legs dangling underneath, he began to rock gently from side to side.

'Just like being on a swing in a playground,' he tried to reassure himself.

The motion started to swing the bell. Little by little the movement grew faster and the bell swung farther. Each time it swung in the direction of the rope it got closer and closer.

Serrion took a deep breath and shuffled off the clapper so that he was now hanging directly underneath the bell, holding onto the leather strap at the full stretch of his arms. With one final swing towards the rope he managed to wrap his legs around it. He squeezed it tightly between his feet. Then, taking one hand gingerly off the leather strap tied to the clapper, he snatched at the rope. His fingers caught it firmly and he let go of the strap with the other hand.

As soon as his weight was transferred back onto the rope, it dropped with a sickening lurch, then held firm as the bell swung right back in the other direction, and lodged itself against the wall of the shaft again. The wooden pulley began to creak ominously above him.

With the last of his energy seeping away, Serrion

climbed back up the last few feet of rope and scrambled onto the platform.

He lay there for some time while his aching muscles tingled and stung as the blood raced back into them.

He waited in the bell tower until it was dark outside. The birds were now all roosting in the eaves of the buildings or up on the rooftops and in high branches. It would be as safe now as ever to make his way back through the city, he thought.

He got to his feet and crept down the steps of the tower.

His journey took a long time. Extreme tiredness and anxiety made him stop to take frequent rests. On every street he paused several times to look around for rish and birds. Thankfully though, he was unchallenged and eventually made his way back to the only place left on Beltheron where he knew he would be safe.

Finally, weeping with relief, Serrion leant upon the handle of the door and fell into an exhausted unconsciousness in the hallway of Matt, Jenn and Helen's house.

To Maraglar

Serrion awoke to find himself propped up on cushions on the huge settee in the front room. Helen fussed around him, constantly asking what she could do to help. Jenn was wiping some of his cuts with a cloth soaked in a strong-smelling liquid.

Like her daughter, who had realised long ago that she felt the same for Serrion even if he was not her cousin, Jenn wasn't concerned at all that this boy was not her real nephew. She had seen him grow up and had always thought of him fondly. 'The important people in our lives are selected with our hearts, not just through the bonds of family,' she had said to Matt one evening.

He had agreed, nodding silently as he thought about the bravery Serrion had shown two years ago when he had helped Helen to escape from the dungeons on Atros. Yes, Serrion had shown his worth, Matt thought solemnly. He deserved their respect and thanks, and whatever help that they could give him now.

'We could shelter you here for the time being,' he said, 'but it makes more sense to get you as far away from your enemies as we can.'

Jenn nodded.

'We have been thinking about what you told us when you went to the Andresens' house,' Matt continued. 'Their study was ransacked, so the person who was there before you couldn't have known what they were looking for.'

'Or they did know *what* it was, but not *where* it was,' Jenn added.

'Either way,' Matt continued, 'that probably means that they weren't working for the Andresens.'

'Do you mean there might be another spy?' Serrion asked. 'Someone we don't know about?'

'It's possible,' Jenn replied. 'But we can't even guess who they are working for or what their motives might be.'

'And as long as there is such uncertainty, we had better make sure you are somewhere safe,' Matt concluded.

Jenn nodded her agreement and disappeared upstairs for a few moments. When she returned she was holding a small sliver of stone. It was a light grey colour, but streaks of bright silver shone out from it, dancing across the room like shafts of moonlight. The whole thing was no bigger than her finger. Neither Helen nor Serrion had ever seen anything quite like it.

'Here,' she pressed the stone into Serrion's hands. 'You should be safe in the place that this takes you to.'

'Where?'

'It is a place where you will not be found,' Matt said.

'On Beltheron?' Helen asked.

'Yes,' her mother replied, 'but far away. It is a place that has been forgotten by most.'

'And where is it?' Serrion repeated. He was starting to panic now. He had not been given any time to consider this. Decisions were being made quickly all around him and he was not even being asked what his opinion was about any of this.

'We're sending you to the lost city of Maraglar,' Matt said. 'It has been deserted for years but will offer you shelter for now.'

Jenn was already holding her own hands over the

stone that she had pushed into Serrion's grasp. He felt it begin to grow warm in his hand. He looked down and saw that the streaks of silver were growing brighter all the time. The room was glowing with a beautiful silvery light.

'The city of Maraglar is vast,' Matt said. 'Make your way to the central tower. It looms over the whole city, and shines with the reflection of the sunlight on its silver walls. You will be as safe hiding in there as anywhere else we can think of.'

In another few moments the pathway was complete and Serrion had disappeared from the room.

They had hardly a moment to think before there was a frantic, loud knocking at the door. It was Cleve Harrow.

'Where is Serrion?' he asked, before he was even fully in the room.

All three members of the Day family looked at each other. Matt spoke up for all of them.

'We sent him away, Cleve. For his own safety.'

'Where? Where have you sent him?'

None of them answered his question.

'Come Matthias, Jenia, how long have we known each other? What you did was right, to get the boy away to safety, but he needs further protection. Birds fly high and far you know, and hunting hawks have eyes much, much keener than ours.'

Matt and Jenn looked at each other. They knew that what the Cleve said was correct. Larena's bird army could not be underestimated. Harrow recognised the expressions on their faces. He knew that he had almost convinced them and pushed on quickly with his argument.

'They could find him easily, even if you think he is hidden well. Let me send one of the pulver to make sure he is protected fully from any danger that might befall.'

Matt broke his wife's gaze and looked down at the

ground for a long moment. Eventually she reached out to grasp his hand. He looked up at her again and gave a small, silent nod.

'Very well Cleve,' he said. 'You have not let us down before. We will trust your judgement in this also.'

Jenn also nodded her head once, very briefly, and then turned away.

It was as if Harrow had breathed a huge sigh of relief. His shoulders relaxed as he reached into the folds of his robe. He brought out a silverscreen.

'That won't work,' Jenn was about to tell Harrow about the interference on the silverscreens, but he silenced her with a wave of his hand. He spoke into it quickly. It crackled and hummed for a moment before Vishan's voice could be recognised.

'Cleve?'

'Vishan, there have been serious developments. Come to Matthias' house as quickly as possible. I have an urgent job for you.'

'Straight away, s....'

The silverscreen gave a click and crackle and then the screen was filled with the same static as Jenn's had been. The Cleve looked at it for a moment warily and suddenly there was Sophia's face staring back at him! Sophia began to laugh but no sound came out of the screen. Jenn and Matt looked over Harrow's shoulder. Jenn gasped with surprise.

'I knew the face was familiar!' she said.

Hurriedly she told her husband and the Cleve about the hazy image in her own silverscreen from the previous day.

They were all caught up in their own thoughts and there was stillness and silence in the room as the three old friends looked at each other. Helen sat alone in the corner, deep in thought.

They waited for several minutes in this tense silence until light footsteps could be heard outside, followed by a quick tap on the door.

Harrow moved across the room and opened the door for Vishan. He merely glanced at the Cleve before his eyes darted around the room. He took in every detail, his training and long experience immediately allowing Vishan to size up any exits for a hasty retreat, or places where possible danger might lurk in the shadows.

Satisfied that all was secure he turned towards Matt and Jenn.

'What has happened? Why am I needed?'

They all explained swiftly. Vishan listened in silence, just nodding occasionally to show he understood the importance of what was going on.

'And where is Serrion now?'

Matt and Jenn didn't reply. They cast a furtive look at each other.

'I must know,' Harrow went on. 'Where is Serrion?'

'We sent him to Maraglar,' Matt said.

'Maraglar, the silver city?' Vishan and Harrow both said together. Their faces showed complete surprise.

'Why there?' Harrow asked. 'What made you think of Maraglar?'

'No one has lived there, or even visited the place for years,' Matt said.

'So we thought that no one would ever think of looking for him there,' Jenn explained. 'And by the looks on both of *your* faces it seems we were right!'

'We told him to head for the central tower,' Matt added.

Harrow thought for a second and then nodded.

'It was a good choice,' he conceded. 'It is doubtful that

either Piotre or Sophia would even remember it after all these years of turning their backs on Beltheron's history. We neglect our heritage and forget our founding principles at our own peril. They would not consider the importance of Maraglar in Beltheron's history.'

'That was exactly what we were thinking,' Jenn said.

Harrow grinned to himself. 'Yes, you made a good decision, but I am afraid Serrion is no longer safe *anywhere*. Now that the Andresens have taken the golden staff who knows to what vile uses it will be put. Serrion needs Vishan to protect and guide him.'

He turned back to Vishan. 'I am sending you to Maraglar,' he said. 'Find Serrion and guard him well. Bring him back to my study here in Beltheron only if you find yourselves in direst danger.'

He turned to the centre of the room. 'Matthias, Jenia, give me one of your vials please so that Vishan can make his return with Serrion.'

Jenn hurried to a drawer and brought back a small bottle. She handed it to Vishan while the Cleve held out his hands towards him and began to speak unfamiliar words under his breath.

A column of brilliant white light sprang up to enclose Vishan. A low humming sound started to fill the room.

The white light grew brighter around the pulver spy until they all had to turn away. Helen placed her hands over her ears as the sound intensified, pressing against her temples like a steadily tightening vice. Why does it always seem louder from the outside?' she wondered briefly as the column of light changed colour to deep red.

After a few more moments the light finally dimmed, the sound ended, and Vishan had gone.

There was a sudden clattering sound of hooves on the cobbles outside the window and a long keening, wailing sound began.

'We acted not a moment too soon,' Harrow murmured under his breath. 'Come, all of you, we must leave. The rish are here.'

They hurried to the back door that led out into the street. There was no time to think. Harrow led the way, with Helen close behind him. Her mum and dad were about to leave as well when there was a cry from overhead. Six hawks came zooming down from the sky towards them. Two flew straight to the open door, forcing Matt to slam it closed again, trapping him and Jenn inside. The others swooped down onto Harrow's shoulders.

With a yell he sent a static burst of blue light up towards them, scattering them back up into the sky in a shower of feathers. Helen cowered into his cloak for comfort.

The attack had cost them vital seconds. The rish rounded the side of the building.

'Follow me,' he hissed, grabbing Helen's shoulder.

'But Mum and Dad -' she began.

'They will be safe within the house. I think it's us they want.'

It looked as if the Cleve was right, for as they hurried away, all of the pursuing rish followed them, leaving Helen's house undisturbed behind them.

Inside the house, Jenn and Matt watched their daughter go. They waited breathlessly for any sound of the rish trying to get into the house. However, after several minutes there was still no sign of threat from outside.

'We must trust in the Cleve now,' Matt said solemnly.

Jenn nodded and went to her husband. They clung tightly to each other, thinking of their daughter.

Sophia held a silverscreen in her hands. There was no static on *this* screen. She could see and hear perfectly well. The screen showed her the interior of Matt and Jenn's house. Her idea to tamper with the silverscreens on Beltheron had been a most useful one. Now she was able to look into any home in the city, and eavesdrop on any conversation she wished.

Sophia curled her lip in disdain for her sister. 'Weak, foolish woman,' she thought to herself about Jenn. 'You chose the wrong side all those years ago.'

Sophia had watched and listened to the entire conversation that had just occurred. 'Maraglar is it?' she murmured under her breath. 'Then that is where I shall go too.'

The Silver City

The city of Maraglar had been deserted for five generations of the Select families. It had been a thriving, busy metropolis. Architecturally it was very different to the mixture of styles and periods that made up the buildings of Beltheron City. The buildings in Maraglar were all made of metal and glass. But apart from this, silver was one of the main materials used on the outside of the buildings. Maraglar had grown up rapidly during an age of great wealth and prosperity, but had come to ruin in the great battle with Gretton Tur, the battle that ended with him being banished to Atros. It had now been many years since anyone had lived there.

The silver buildings of Maraglar were slim and tall. They reached proudly upwards towards the skies like icicles or gleaming swords. Serrion had to shield his eyes several times as he made his way through the deserted streets. The sunlight glanced from one building to the next reminding him for a moment of the way the mirrors of the time tower in Beltheron City reflected onto each other.

He thought of that day two years ago when Orianna had shown him around Beltheron and told him about the time tower. With a sharp pang in his chest he realised how much he missed her. How had she taken the news of their mother's death, he wondered. He wished he could be with her. They could at least help to comfort each other. He felt terribly lonely and exposed in the cold reflected light.

Serrion continued through the streets. He saw that they were constructed from large metal plates, like oversized tiles, instead of cobbles or tarmac. This hard metallic surface showed his own reflection as he looked down.

In the distance he could see the building that Matt and Jenn had told him about. It rose far higher than any other construction in Maraglar, dwarfing everything else around it like a massive cruise liner surrounded by small fishing vessels. His view of the top of the tower was hazy because wispy clouds floated across the pale grey sky.

Because of the scale of the surrounding buildings, Serrion knew that the tower must still be some distance away. Seeing such a huge tower so far off made him realise just how vast the city of Maraglar must be.

So big a place... And so silent.

There was no one else in this whole city except him. This thought only served to increase his loneliness and isolation as he moved through the streets.

'Matt and Jenn were right,' he thought to himself. 'No one could find me in such a place.' He didn't know whether to be comforted or alarmed by such a thought.

He trudged on as the afternoon light grew brighter and hotter. His muscles still ached and he felt bruised and battered from his fight with the brannoch, but he knew that he had to continue.

The tower was now directly in front of him. It seemed that it was now only a couple of streets away, at the other side of just one more block of buildings.

First though, he came out into a wide, open concourse. It was about the size of a football pitch. There was a river running through the centre with a smooth, gleaming bridge arching over it. The bridge looked slippery. There was no handrail. The river wound away as far as he could see in either direction. He could see no other way to get across. The tower was now tantalisingly close on the other side.

Serrion gave a sigh of resignation. There was nothing else for it. As dangerous as it looked, he would have to try to cross the narrow bridge.

Vishan arrived in Maraglar city in a flash of light. He squinted his eyes as it bounced backwards and forwards off the smooth sides of the silver metallic buildings.

Harrow's pathway had set Vishan down directly in front of the broad steps of the tower.

He knew he must have arrived here only twenty or thirty minutes behind Serrion. Matt and Jenn's pathway could have deposited Serrion anywhere in this huge city. It could be anything between five minutes and three hours before the boy found his way here. Vishan realised that he might be in for a long wait.

Vishan leaned back as he looked up at the tower. Its top storeys disappeared into the misty clouds. His cloak swirled around his shoulders as a sudden wind blew through the city. It made an eerie whistling sound that cut through the silence of the deserted streets. To Vishan's ears it sounded like the moans of soldiers wounded on the battlefield.

He began to climb the steps to the base of the silver tower to wait for Serrion to arrive.

Sophia wasted no time. As soon as she had heard of Serrion's destination through the silverscreen she hurried to her husband to inform him of these new developments. Both had agreed that it was best if she followed him straight away to the silver city.

'Dispose of the boy once and for all,' Piotre said with a snarl. 'But take care, my beloved. If the wretch can escape a brannoch, then he might be more wily and dangerous than we had supposed.'

Serrion approached the bridge. Even close up it seemed dangerously narrow. The water was flowing swiftly in the river below. It reflected the pale silver colours of the buildings that rose into the sky all around. Serrion realised that in different circumstances, all this would be extremely beautiful to look at. He took a deep breath and placed his right foot on the bridge.

There was just enough width for him to position his whole foot onto it without the sides of his trainers hanging over the edge. Luckily it was not as slippery as it appeared. Even so it felt as if he were about to step out onto a tightrope without a safety net below him.

Gradually he made his way safely to the other side.

'Thank goodness it wasn't wet underfoot,' he thought to himself. Relieved that he was now so close to his destination, he broke into a run to get to the tower.

As he approached he thought he saw someone sitting on the steps of the building. He slowed to a halt. Matt and Jenn had told him the city was deserted, so who could this be?

The figure rose to his feet and waved. With a huge surge of relief, Serrion recognised the friendly features of Vishan and hurried towards him.

They were so involved in greeting each other that they did not see the flash in the air near to the bridge, or the appearance of a woman in a deep purple cloak and waves of long dark brown hair flowing over her shoulders. She watched them disappear into the building below the tower and started to follow them.

Decisions and Promises

The small bones of the steasle were now scattered around the glowing embers of the fire. They were all that was left of Parenon's and Orianna's supper. They had been deep in close conversation for over an hour.

Parenon was gazing at Orianna. His eyes gleamed bright and were focused intently on her face.

She felt herself flush red and her heart felt that it was being slowly squeezed by a heavy pair of hands.

Then Parenon's own hands were reaching out towards her. In one of the bravest things that the young pulver had ever done he leant towards Orianna and gently brushed her cheek with his lips.

Orianna touched his face with her fingertips. She had never felt so many strange emotions all at one time. Hope, fear, excitement, were all confused together with the deep sorrow she felt for her mother. She returned his kiss briefly.

'They must not win,' Parenon said. 'The Andresens must not be victorious. We cannot let them.'

'You are right,' she said. 'There is so much good in our worlds, so much to live and fight for. I will stand with you, Parenon. Together we will go back to Beltheron City and do whatever we must.'

'Even if it means facing terrible danger?' he replied.

Orianna nodded. 'If I am by your side it will not seem so frightening.'

'No,' he shook his head. 'It is my task to protect you. I cannot put you in the path of even more danger. I *will* not.'

'I am not going to run and hide in the shadows any longer, Parenon,' she said to him.

'But the Cleve said that we...'

She placed her fingers against his lips to silence him.

'Listen to me,' she said. 'I have lost so much, but I know there is still much to save, and to protect. And I want to stand alongside *you* in order to try to save it.'

They clasped each other's hands tightly. Both grinned foolishly.

'There is nothing I can do here,' Orianna said after a few moments of thought. 'I am filled with too many thoughts of my mother. I need to work, I need to be busy so that I can try to stop these feelings from overwhelming me.'

Parenon nodded. He understood perfectly.

'I have to get back to my books,' she said. 'The pages that Cleve Harrow showed me in this,' she held up the volume that he had given them, 'have given me an idea.'

She began sprinkling droplets from a vial onto the book, and within moments the two of them were travelling through the swirling lights of a pathway.

There was no sign of Harrow when the two of them returned to his stone tower in Beltheron City. The book had done just as the Cleve had said it would and returned them directly to his study.

Orianna immediately began scouring the shelves. There was a particular book she was looking for.

Parenon looked on as Orianna began scribbling the words down into a small leather-bound notebook. As she wrote she repeated the words under her breath. They made no sense to Parenon. In fact, they sounded like a foreign language to him. Something like: *'Imperilar rabensmancer Landeyeda.'* She whispered them over and over to herself, as if learning lines for a play. *'Imperilar rabensmancer Landeyeda.'* And then: *'Toto derelictum in scrupulor mantasis.'*

Finally she looked up. She smiled happily at Parenon. Seeing him standing there made her feel brave.

'Come on,' she said. 'We need to get to the great hall.'

The Real Spy?

Serrion thought that he was probably as relaxed and comfortable as it was possible to be after such recent dangers and escapes. He and Vishan were resting on soft cushions. They were placed around a huge fireplace on the ground floor of the tower in Maraglar. Vishan had lit a fire from old logs and twigs that still sat in a silver barrel on the broad hearth. The warmth of the flickering flames calmed his nerves as well as warming his fingers and cold toes.

They had been talking for some time, keeping their voices low, even though it was unlikely that they would carry far through the corridors and out into the early evening air.

'It is very difficult to lose a loved one – especially a parent,' Vishan was saying. 'When it happened to me, I felt hollow - dead inside – for months.'

Serrion didn't reply for a long time. He stared into the flames, poking at the glowing embers with a thick twig. Vishan didn't push him for a response. He let the silence hang around them, leaving Serrion with his thoughts.

After couple of minutes Vishan spoke again.

'I felt guilty as well as being scared and angry about what had happened. Why should I still live and breathe when they could not? Could I have changed things? Could I have done anything to save my father on that day?

Serrion continued staring into the fire. He recognised

all that Vishan was telling him. The same feelings were etched into his own heart. He constantly asked himself the same questions. Was there something he could have done to save Korellia?

'What happened to your father?' he asked Vishan.

'We were living near to Atros City,' Vishan began.

'You all *lived* there? On Atros! Your whole family?'

'Yes. About twenty five to thirty years ago many families began to set up homes and villages there. Gretton Tur was still under strict controls – house arrest I suppose you could call it – and my father was a pulver captain who was in charge of a group of men who kept watch over him. We all considered that Tur was safe at that time. No one guessed what trickery he had been plotting.'

'When I first met Cleve Harrow he told me something of it,' Serrion said. 'How Tur built up support over the years and began to gain control on Atros.'

'That's right,' Vishan nodded grimly. 'Slowly and secretly he won minds and souls to his cause. His magic was always strong and even in exile under close watch we should have guessed that his powers would not desert him.'

The pulver agent gave a deep sigh and Serrion saw his shoulders sag with weary resignation.

'In any case it is too late now for regrets and blame. The fact remains that we did not manage to prevent him from working his malice afresh on a new group of people.'

'So how did this affect you and your family?'

Vishan stared into the fire silently for a while before he answered.

'One day I was visiting Atros City with my mother, sister and brother. There was a special presentation being made to the men in my father's band of pulver. We had been given special seats of honour to watch the presentation, because my father was the captain.'

Vishan was obviously distressed by the memories. Serrion could tell that it was difficult for him to continue.

'I remember being so thrilled and excited on that day; so proud of my father.

'But before the presentation could take place, there was a huge explosion on the field where my father and the rest of the pulver were standing.'

Vishan paused. He took a deep breath and then said quite simply, 'None of the pulver survived the blast.

'It happened to many others as well. On other occasions. You know of Tarawen, who works for us with the rebels on Atros?' Serrion nodded. 'The story of his family is just as tragic as mine.'

Serrion turned away. The things that Vishan was telling him did not take away the pain or the anger that he felt. However, knowing that others had gone through similar experiences, that others felt the same way he did, made the pain easier to deal with.

He realised that he was getting sleepy. His thoughts began to wander. Memories of his mother were mingled with all the other things that had been happening to him lately.

Then, as his eyelids started to droop, one particular thought came creeping into his mind: what Matt had been saying about the ransacked study in his old house in London. *Someone* not connected to the Andresen family must have been in London on the same day as him. That person had taken information before he, Serrion, could discover it. And if they weren't connected with the Andresen family then they must be from Beltheron itself, Serrion reasoned. And... and... He started dozing as the thought wormed its way through his sleepy mind ...And *someone* from Beltheron must have been in London on that day to help him escape from Bargoth and Lathe.

He was suddenly wide awake again. He had come back to the same question time and time again. Was the person who ransacked the study the same one who had helped him, he wondered?

But why would anyone who wanted to save him also wish to take secrets and information from the house? If they were on his side, and wanted to keep him safe, what information did they want to keep for themselves? With a sickening lurch in his stomach, Serrion began to wonder if the secrets and lies would ever end.

He was still considering this when he saw a particularly bright red ember glowing at the very edge of the fire. He shook his head to clear it. 'Of course you can see red, you fool,' he thought to himself, 'you're staring into a fire!'

But the red got brighter.

It looked different to the other glowing pieces of wood. This one was taking on a more rounded, solid form even as he watched.

He could not hesitate any longer. It must be a warning.

'Vishan,' he began. 'You probably think this is crazy but...'

Before he could finish speaking, the tall window of the hall shattered.

Five rish leapt through. They held long, sharp scimitars in their hands.

Vishan and Serrion were both on their feet in an instant. Vishan's hand was already inside his robe, drawing his sword from its leather scabbard.

Serrion's head spun. *Someone* must have talked and let the rish know that they were here. It was impossible that they could have found them so quickly by mere chance.

'Follow me!' Vishan hissed thickly in his ear. The pulver ran towards the door. Serrion still hesitated, even though he could hear the high, whinnying shrieks of the rish as they raced down the corridor towards them.

Questions spilled and tumbled through his head.

'How have they found us?' he asked Vishan. 'Who could have told them?'

Vishan had been wondering the same thing. Then, suddenly he realised.

'Harrow's silverscreen!' he groaned in dismay as he ran. 'The Andresens must have intercepted the signal!'

Serrion stopped in his tracks. Harrow's silverscreen? It was unlike the Cleve to make such a simple mistake.

'Come *on!*' yelled Vishan. He was almost at the door now and Serrion saw the pulver throw out his hand and a green light flashed from it. The door swung open, giving them a clear escape. Serrion looked at Vishan, amazed.

'Yes, I can do that as well,' Vishan said as he saw the look on his face.

Vishan shared the same skill as he did! He could open doorways too, but he did it with a flashing green light!

Serrion struggled to remember why this seemed so important.

A green light.

A green light like the one that had flashed by the gate on the London street to throw Bargoth and Lathe off balance. A green light in London only twenty minutes after he had discovered the ransacked study in the Andresens' house.

Suddenly Serrion knew. As he followed Vishan through the silver corridors, memories and suspicions fell into place and in a moment he realised everything.

It was *Vishan* who had already been in London that day when Serrion had travelled the pathway. It was Vishan who had used the powers given him by the Cleve to open a pathway and get to the Andresen house first.

Vishan would then have had time to search the study

to remove that secret – whatever it was - and hide it. But what *was* that secret and how had it made Vishan turn traitor to Beltheron? How had he managed to trick Harrow, who believed in the pulver spy so completely?

But even as Serrion was thinking this through, he knew that it didn't make sense. If Vishan *was* a traitor then why would he be trying to save him now? Why would Vishan tell the rish where they were and then risk his own life helping him to escape? Why hadn't he just killed Serrion himself earlier, when he had had plenty of opportunity?

It just didn't make sense for Vishan to be the spy.

As he was working all this out, Serrion realised that Vishan was speaking to him again. The pulver had seen his hesitation and knew he had to get him moving.

'You can trust me, Serrion,' he was saying. 'You *know* you can trust me. Cleve Harrow himself sent me here.'

Cleve Harrow.

Cleve Harrow had sent Vishan to find him. Vishan always followed the Cleve's orders. Had the Cleve sent Vishan to London that day to ransack the study? And if he had, then the same question applied to the Cleve too. What had Cleve Harrow wanted to keep secret from him?

There was a triumphant howl behind them.

Serrion realised he had no choice; he had to follow Vishan. His mind writhing in indecision and anguish, Serrion hurled himself across the hall and followed Vishan into the street outside.

The Revelation

Harrow and Helen made their way back to Harrow's private study in the library buildings of Beltheron. They had managed to slip away from the rish on one of the side streets.

It was clear that Harrow had left the library in a hurry, as there were papers scattered everywhere. It reminded Helen of the papers thrown around in the Andresens' study in London. Then she saw something else which made her think of that day. Piled up on Harrow's table was the row of six purple books that they had brought back with them.

Harrow was saying something to her, but she wasn't listening any more. Her attention was completely fixed on the books. There was something different about them. What was it?

Harrow was still speaking, but she didn't hear the words. Helen didn't even notice that he had moved up behind her. She was too busy counting the books. Suddenly she gasped.

There weren't six of them now. There were seven.

From the angle that she was standing, she couldn't quite make out the silver writing on the spines. Slowly she began to move sideways, to get a closer view. In a moment the writing on the top book became clear. In a whisper that seemed loud in the suddenly silent room she read out the single word on the book's spine: '*Desolatum.*'

'That's right, my dear,' Harrow spoke softly behind her.

She spun around, still confused as to what was happening.

'The missing book! *You* had it all the time?'

'No,' he replied. 'Vishan took it from the Andresens' study for me, only minutes before young Serrion got there. I couldn't allow him to find it you see.'

'No,' Helen replied. 'I don't see.'

'I tried to talk Serrion out of going back to his old home, but he and Orianna just wouldn't let the idea rest.'

'But why? Why couldn't he see what the book said?'

Harrow smiled wistfully to himself before answering.

'It wasn't just the book itself,' he began to explain. 'It was the rather silly handwritten note in the front pages.'

'A note? Handwritten by whom?'

He smiled again. 'By me, my dear.'

Helen's mouth dropped open. 'A note for the Andresens?'

He nodded. 'It laid out all our plans. Or, I should say, what we wanted the Andresens to *believe* were our plans.'

Helen now spoke very slowly. 'I think you should tell me exactly what it is you are talking about.'

Harrow considered for a long moment before he answered. When he did speak his voice was calm and controlled.

'You know how important Serrion has become to us?' he began. 'You must know the terrible consequences for all of us if we fail?'

Harrow took a deep breath, a corner of his mind uncertain, even now, about exactly how much to tell the young woman. Then, with a sigh of resignation, he continued.

'The year before Serrion was born, the great seer T'yuq Tinyaz summoned me to her lake in the caves underneath

Beltheron City. T'yuq Tinyaz had beheld an image of the boy who is carved onto the golden staff.'

'Serrion,' Helen said. It was a statement, not a question.

Harrow nodded. 'Yes, it was Serrion. T'yuq Tinyaz had seen him in a vision before he had even been born; she knew who he would become. She saw in that same moment the whole of the part that he would play in our history. *Right up to this moment and beyond*. It was one of her clearest visions and she told me all of it.'

Harrow paused again, looking intently into Helen's eyes. 'Do you understand me, my dear? Do you realise now what I am telling you? T'yuq Tinyaz told me *all of it*.'

Helen swallowed hard. Tears began to swim in her eyes with the enormity of what Harrow was beginning to say to her.

'You… you *knew*?' she stammered. 'You have *always* known what was going to happen?'

Harrow nodded slowly.

'Yes. Before you and Serrion were even born. Ungolin and I met with the seer and discussed what we had to do. She looked into several possible futures and the one with the best outcome for us all started with Korellia's little boy being switched for Jacques Andresen.'

Helen was shaking her head in disbelief at what the Cleve was telling her.

'It was me who sent one of my agents to Piotre and Sophia,' he continued. 'I told him to suggest to the two of them that it would be most useful if their son could be trained by Gretton Tur in secret from an early age. He told them he would find a baby about the same age as Jacques, to replace him, so that no one would notice. He was my most trusted agent, and he managed to trick them into this course of action which would have such huge consequences for us all.'

'Vishan?' she guessed. 'Was Vishan the agent you sent?'

He nodded. 'Yes, Vishan was a young pulver at the time. His head was still filled with anger at what had happened to his family on Atros. He was eager to help bring about the destruction of our enemies.'

Helen felt a coldness creep through her body. She shivered with the shocking realisation of what this all meant.

'So it was *your* idea,' she whispered under her breath. 'Not theirs; not Gretton Tur's, not Uncle Piotre's or Aunt Sophia's! It was *your* idea to take Serrion from the very beginning!'

Questions were now racing through her mind.

'But how did you get Piotre and Sophia to believe Vishan? Why should they do as he said? Why would they agree to give up their own son to Gretton Tur?'

'Vishan had been in place for several months by this time,' the Cleve replied. 'He had been working as a double agent, feeding the Andresens with false information. And, by doing this of course, Vishan had also been misleading Gretton Tur himself.'

'So Vishan had convinced them that he was working against you and Ungolin?'

Harrow nodded. 'That's right. And after a while it was not difficult to convince them of the value of our plan.'

'I suppose Vishan was the 'advisor' you talked about that day in your study, when I asked you why Piotre and Sophia would still have a home on Earth?'

Harrow nodded. 'Yes, Vishan convinced them that there were those on Atros who could not be trusted with secrets.' He smiled at the memory. 'Vishan played his part brilliantly all along. He also told the Andresens that he had persuaded Ungolin there was no sign of them anywhere in London, and that no further investigations were to be made there. No wonder they chose their old home as a refuge.'

'But… but… Now hang on!' Helen was getting angrier by the moment. Yet another thought had just occurred to her. 'If all these things you're telling me are true then that means you must have known about the Andresens all along. You must have known that they would agree to the plan.' She was jabbing her finger at him accusingly now. 'You couldn't have come up with that idea unless you yourself already knew that Piotre and Sophia were working for Gretton Tur!'

Harrow nodded. 'Yes, Ungolin and I had both known for years.'

Helen was furious now. 'So if you knew all this, for so many years, if you *always* knew that my Uncle Piotre and Aunt Sophia were the traitors, then why didn't you just arrest them or something? You could have locked them up so they couldn't do any more harm.'

Harrow smiled thinly down at her. The smile was not friendly, but instead it seemed to say, 'Oh you poor innocent young child! How little you know about the dealings of the real world!'

'We *could* have arrested them, as you say,' he agreed. 'And, no doubt, that would have worked for a while. We would have stopped Piotre and Sophia and slowed the progress of the Wild Lord for a short time. But instead of that, by using the vision of future events given to us by T'yuq Tinyaz, we realised that here was an opportunity to destroy him forever!'

There was now an ardent gleam in the Cleve's face. His voice had risen slightly to a new pitch of excitement as he carried on explaining his actions. 'Through the seer's visions we could see a way to use the Andresen family to bring about Gretton Tur's ultimate ruin!

'T'yuq Tinyaz knew how vital Serrion's role was for the future of all of us,' Harrow continued. 'She foresaw what he could become given our support and help.'

Helen glared at him. 'Help and support? Huh! I call it interference!'

The Cleve was undeterred; he carried on speaking steadily, holding Helen's gaze.

'Serrion himself was never a member of the Select Families by birth,' Harrow said. 'We *selected that role for him*. In a way that makes him even more important.'

Helen grunted with disgust.

'Don't be sharp with me young woman!' Harrow's voice was suddenly harsh and angry. 'Ungolin himself understood what needed to be done.'

'So you *both* knew? You and Lord Ungolin both had a part in this! How could you use a child in that way? At the time, Serrion was still just a baby.'

'There are reasons that were much more important than the welfare of a single child.'

'I can't believe that.' Helen's face was hard and angry.

'By sacrificing one we could save many.'

'But there had to be a different way. Using people like that, causing so much hurt and heartbreak is just evil! It turns you into the thing you are supposed to be fighting.' Helen's voice was now beginning to come in ragged sobs. She struggled to get her breath and lifted a hand to wipe angry tears from her cheek.

'There has to be a point where we stop,' she said. 'Because if we don't stop, if we all ignore what's going on, or if we just agree to let you do things like that, then it makes us no better than Gretton Tur himself.'

She drew herself upright, looking defiantly into Harrow's yellowy-green eyes.

'I'm going to tell him,' she said in a quiet, determined

voice. 'I'm going to go to Serrion at the first opportunity I can get, and I'm going to tell him what you have done to him and his family.'

'No!'

Harrow's arm shot out suddenly and he grabbed her arm. His fingers dug deep into her flesh so that she gasped with shock. As she looked up at him, she realised she had never seen him looking so fierce and determined.

Harrow's voice came out in no more than a whisper.

'He must *not* be told!' he hissed. 'It could ruin everything! Serrion is growing into a fine, worthy young man. He is so valuable to us. We cannot afford for him to lose his faith in us, especially now. He *must not* be told!'

He was still gripping her arm as he spoke, twisting it now so that Helen was almost tipped off her feet. She pulled away from the Cleve, snapping at him in fury and pain.

'You knew what you had done to him was wrong, otherwise you wouldn't have tried to hide your tracks by sending Vishan out to ransack the Andresens' house.'

'It *had* to be kept secret, you stupid girl! If anyone found out it would have ruined everything.'

There was a note of pleading in Harrow's voice now. He knew he was losing her. 'If Serrion had found out it would have destroyed him.'

Helen had already turned away from him. Tears stabbed at her eyes.

'And if he found out now it would still destroy him,' Harrow added quietly.

'I can't listen to you anymore,' she sobbed. 'I can't even look at you. You have betrayed *all of us,* everyone on Beltheron. Well I won't be a part of this. I'm going to find Serrion right now and tell him what you've done.'

'No!' Harrow's yell was so loud and violent that it

stopped Helen in her tracks. She turned back to face him once more.

Harrow's voice was clear and determined.

'T'yuq Tinyaz foresaw another possible future too,' he said slowly. 'She saw a future where you *did* tell Serrion about all of this. When he discovered what we had done he turned against us. In *that* future, he... he...' Harrow dropped his head and stared at the ground.

'What?' Helen asked. She took a couple of slow steps towards the Cleve. 'What will Serrion do if he finds out the truth?'

Harrow did not answer her. He just looked at her in silence for what seemed like a very long time. Eventually Helen felt that she could not meet that gaze any longer. She turned away.

'How far would *you* go Yelenia?' he asked her at last. Her old, Belthronic name now sounded distasteful and horrid in his mouth. 'You have already achieved so much. How much further would you go; how much more would you do for something that you *really* believed in?'

'Not that,' she whispered. 'Not what you did.'

Her head was bent low down onto her chest. She was still turned away from him. 'I couldn't betray a friend like that.'

Harrow gave a short, bitter laugh behind her.

'Still so young,' he chided. 'Sometimes Ungolin and I have to make the choice between a friend and the whole land. It is never easy.'

He went silent again for a moment. Helen still gazed at the ground in front of her, trying to come to terms with what all this meant. In the thickness of the atmosphere that hung between them, Harrow spoke up again – his voice now more urgent and harsh than before.

'Sometimes it is no choice at all,' he said. 'It is no choice because there is no alternative, no other possible course of action. But even so, I am sorry lady Yelenia, I am so, so sorry for what I have to do now.'

Something about the tone of his voice made her turn before he had finished speaking. She saw him raise his arm towards her; saw the pain and pity flash through his eyes for a second. Then, as if from far away, she heard her own voice begin to scream as Cleve Harrow's arm shot out and a blaze of red fire sped from his fingers towards her.

The Bridge

The silver streets reflected the grey light of the cloudy sky. The first drops of rain began to fall as Vishan and Serrion raced forwards towards the narrow bridge that crossed the river.

The rish were in hot pursuit. Vishan wondered whether to turn and fight, to give Serrion more time and a better chance to create a pathway to escape. With this in mind he took the vial that Jenn had given to him. He pushed it towards Serrion's hand as they ran.

'Don't wait for me,' he said.

'What?'

'Just get over the bridge. I'll deal with this.'

'But...'

'There's no time to argue my friend. It's an order.'

Serrion saw the look on the pulver's face and knew that arguments were no use. He was deadly serious.

Taking the vial from Vishan's outstretched hand he sped on towards the bridge as Vishan spun around to face their attackers.

In the last few moments the rain had suddenly become fast and heavy. It was now slicing down diagonally. Serrion was looking down at his feet to watch his step on the slippery surface as he ran up onto the slick surface of the narrow bridge. His attention was so focused on where he was placing his steps that he almost bumped into the figure standing in the middle of the bridge's arc directly in front of him.

He cried out in surprise and alarm. Balancing as best he could, he raised his eyes to look at the figure. Standing there, dressed in a long flowing purple robe was a woman he knew so well, yet didn't know at all. Her hard face stared back at him and a cold smile curled around her thin lips. Sophia Andresen.

'Good evening, my boy,' she said. Her voice was teasing and cruel.

Serrion felt a hammering in his chest that was a mixture of anger, frustration, and a deep, longing sorrow. He gulped thickly to choke back the emotion he felt rising in his throat. The rain slashed against his face and helped to disguise the tears that were brimming in his eyes. With his own voice cracking he replied simply.

'I am not your boy.'

There was silence between them for several moments. Neither broke the other's gaze. If you looked closely, you might have spotted the smallest tremor of emotion, maybe even regret, around Sophia Andresen's mouth. It only lasted a moment though, if it had ever been there at all. Perhaps it was just the way the rain ran around her lips.

Serrion felt ridiculous. Time after time over the last two years he had wanted violent revenge on this woman who now stood in front of him. But he found he could do nothing. Here he was, cold, hungry, soaking wet through, probably only minutes from death, and yet all he wanted now was to talk to her.

'How? How could you do it?' he asked.

'It was necessary,' she said. 'We needed you as part of a much larger plan.'

'Didn't you feel anything at all about the people you were hurting?'

She merely smiled.

'Tell me!' he shouted. 'Did you not even feel sorry *once* for what you had done?'

The rain could not disguise his tears any longer; they flowed freely down his cheeks. He made no attempt to wipe them away.

'And did... did you...' he gulped again. He *had* to find out. 'Did you ever even care for me at *all*?'

A different light came into her eyes, but was immediately dimmed again.

'Did you?' he repeated softly. 'Please, I *have* to know.'

She opened her mouth briefly as if to answer him.

But before she had a chance to say the words that were beginning to form on her lips, Serrion felt himself struck in the small of the back by something heavy. He grunted in pain and sank to his knees, grabbing the narrow bridge with both hands to keep his balance. A shadowy figure leapt over him and struck Sophia, knocking her off the bridge.

Serrion clung on and looked down into the water. There, being swept away swiftly by the strong current, were the struggling bodies of Vishan and Sophia. They tumbled over and over, locked together in battle, as they were carried into the deeper water in the middle of the river.

Serrion risked another brief look behind him. He saw that Vishan had done his work well. The fallen bodies of the pursuing rish were scattered around on the ground close to the bridge. He turned back to look at the water.

They had now been drawn under the violently rippling surface. Serrion could make out the blue of Vishan's cloak, billowing beneath the water. Sophia's hand appeared briefly through the foam. Then there was a bright flash of light and a small eruption of spray where they had been.

He squinted through the driving rain, but there was

now no sign of either of them.

'Vishan!' Serrion yelled wildly. 'Vishaaan!'

And then, after a gasp of breath, he called again, just one despairing word into the driving desolation of rain.

'Mum!'

Helen's Escape

Helen turned away and threw herself to the ground. In one long, fluid movement she rolled over the rough tiles on the floor as the blast of fire from Harrow's fingers crackled in the air above her.

The door to the library was only a few metres away but she knew without having to look behind her that Harrow would already be aiming to fire at her again. Whimpering in fear and outrage that this could be happening to her, she twisted again, this time rolling back in the other direction.

She had guessed right. Her instincts and timing were perfect. Just as she rolled, the tiles where she had been lying a moment before shattered. Jagged bits of broken tile stung her face. She closed her eyes and jumped to her feet.

Her last movements had brought her closer to the door. She was now only a few paces away.

The door was still closed however, and she knew that it opened inwards. It would take too long to pull at the heavy brass handle. An idea came to her. Her last chance!

Letting her Select instincts guide her again she took one more racing step towards the door until she was directly in front of it. In her mind she could sense the Cleve raise his arm a third time and gather his power. After two strikes of energy so close together, Helen guessed that he would need an extra second to fire off a third blast.

Listening intently for the hissing crackle as the fire left

his fingers, she hurled herself down at the last moment. Fire fizzed above her, so close that it singed her hair and she felt the scorching heat on her face.

But her plan worked.

The bolt of fire hit the old oaken door right in the centre and it splintered. The wood was blasted outwards by Cleve Harrow's rage.

Helen hauled herself back onto her feet. Plunging through the remains of the door she raced down the corridor. Luckily it curved away to the left and in just a few paces she was out of Cleve Harrow's firing line. She ducked right, and then left again. After her many visits here in the past she could remember the route through the maze of corridors down to the front doors of the library buildings. But she could still hear footsteps hurrying behind her.

Helen's thoughts ran on ahead. Instead of taking the next corridor on her left – which would have taken her straight to the wide staircase and down to the street – she turned to a door on her right. She tried the handle.

Luckily the door was not locked. Heaving it wide open she then ran past it and ducked behind a large tapestry on the wall a few metres further on. She tried to remain motionless in her hiding place but her breath came in ragged gasps through fear and exertion as she waited.

From the gap between the tapestry and the wall she saw Harrow run through the corridor leading to the staircase. For a moment she thought that he would not see the open door, and carry on pursuing her. But at the last moment he paused. Helen watched as he stood in thought.

'Go on!' thought Helen. 'Go in!'

Harrow took a final look down the long corridor before making his decision. He turned and plunged through the open doorway.

'It worked,' Helen said to herself. 'He fell for it. He

went the wrong way.'

She ran out from behind her hiding pace and quickly and quietly made her way down the staircase.

There were two guards at the doorway out to the main piazza. Helen ignored them, racing through the doors and onto the streets of Beltheron City as their shouts echoed behind her.

But who could she trust, Helen wondered? Even in her haste to escape, her mind was still turning over what she had just heard. Harrow and Ungolin! Was there no one left at all who would help her? With a stifling, cold chill her thoughts ran on to her own parents. What about them? Serrion had lived his whole life in a lie – what if she had too? What if even her own parents couldn't be trusted?

It *couldn't* be true, she argued to herself. She knew her parents had worked against Gretton Tur and the evils of Atros. Deep down inside herself she just *knew* how much they hated what had been done to Serrion and all the lies that had been told.

But what if they had felt they *had* to go along with it? Just as Harrow and Ungolin believed in what they had done, what if her own mum and dad had been persuaded to join in with their plan, convinced that there was no other way to achieve a final victory? Would they, *could* they have kept that a secret from her for all these years?

But even as these treacherous suspicions sprang up, she knew in the very core of her heart that they were false. She pushed the doubts down again. No. she would not believe that. If she lost faith in her own family now, then she might as well give in completely, turn around and hand herself in to the guards of the great hall.

She carefully made her way home through the streets of Beltheron. She had never felt the need to be more cautious or watchful in her life. There was danger behind her in the shape of Cleve Harrow, danger above her because of the birds, and danger ahead of her at every turn, because of the bands of rish and pulver fighting each other. There was also a strict curfew that kept everyone indoors for safety. That meant that if even if she met a pulver, she would still be in trouble, possibly even arrested, for being outside and breaking the law.

At least most of the birds now seemed to be at rest, she thought. She could see them roosting on fence posts and roofs all around her. In spite of her urgency she slowed herself down even more, so that she would not wake the creatures.

Apart from the birds, the streets were deserted. The curfew held. She did not come upon any groups of rish, and in spite of her fears, her journey home was quite uneventful.

Once she had to duck into a doorway as two pulver walked past on the opposite side of the street, and once a bird sitting on a gatepost close by her shoulder squawked suddenly making her heart leap into her mouth. She shrank back into the shadows. Would the bird sound an alarm and wake the others nearby? Centimetre by centimetre she edged past it, not daring to take her eyes off its face. But the bird merely resettled itself back onto its perch. It was obviously contented and not worried about her. Fluffing up its feathers the bird settled back into sleep.

On she went without any further problems. But when she finally arrived back at her house, Helen's heart sank.

Harrow was already there. He stood in front of her front door. He was looking around anxiously. As she watched, a small group of pulver came out of the house and began to consult with the Cleve.

How had he managed to get them all there before her, she wondered? Then she saw the two large cylindrical buggies hovering a metre above the ground at the side of the house. The buggies were long, sleek and grey and looked very fast. Pulver rarely used the flying ships to get around, and she had never seen Harrow riding on one before.

'They must think of me as a really serious threat if they are using them now,' she thought to herself.

Each one of the flying machines looked large enough to carry at least four people. There were three pulver standing outside, talking to Harrow, so that meant there could possibly be another four or five inside the house.

Helen cowered in the cover of the bushes. She strained her ears and could just about hear what Harrow was saying to the pulver.

'You are certain that Matthias and Jenia were not here?' he asked.

The pulver nodded in reply.

'Rish attacked here earlier. Was there a sign of struggle?'

This time the pulver shook his head. 'Cannish said that he had seen them running to one of the houses over there,' he waved his hand in the direction of a row of houses that Helen knew well. Friends of her mum and dad lived there.

Helen breathed a huge sigh of relief. At least her parents were safe and had escaped the rish.

Harrow dismissed this news. He spoke again to the guard. 'It is of the utmost importance that we find the girl Yelenia,' he said urgently. 'She has turned against us. She has stolen secret documents from Lord Ungolin's study and means to take them to Piotre Andresen.'

Helen's mouth dropped in shock to hear the lies that

the Cleve was telling about her.

'She must not be allowed to escape from Beltheron,' he continued. 'Search the house for any kron, or small vials of liquid you can find and bring them to me. I will go to find the girl's parents.'

Harrow turned away and his gaze passed over the very spot where Helen was hiding. The look of hatred and anger in his yellowy-green eyes made her quail with fear. If she had held any doubt that Harrow could be persuaded against what he was doing, it disappeared now. She had never seen anyone looking as terrifying as this man that she used to trust with her life. Now one look at those eyes told her that Cleve Harrow would kill her at the very first opportunity.

Helen felt a wave of nausea pass through her and felt for a moment that she might be sick. She realised that she must have made a noise of dismay and despair. But Harrow still made no sign of having heard or seen her. She slunk even further back into the bush and began to creep away towards the side of the house, furthest away from where the others were standing.

On this side of the house there was a large water barrel standing next to the wall just under one of the windows. To reach it Helen knew that she would have to run across an open patch of the yard without any hope of cover. If either the pulver guards or Harrow happened to look in her direction she would be spotted immediately.

She glanced back towards where they were gathered. Another small group of guards had just arrived and the Cleve was beginning to direct them towards the front door. There would be even more of them inside the house at any moment!

Harrow's attention was still with this new batch of pulver. It was now or never, she realised.

Taking a deep breath Helen leapt from her hiding place and sprinted across the open yard. With three strides to go she leapt towards the barrel. She scrabbled with her hands to clamber up and in a moment she was squeezing through the narrow gap. Half way through the window she lost her balance and tipped headfirst into the room. Helen grunted as she landed heavily on her right shoulder. A sharp, intense pain shot up through her arm but she stifled the cry that threatened to break from her lips and reveal her location.

Rolling onto her knees she cradled her elbow and rubbed her arm vigorously. She could hear the pulver moving around in the very next room! How long did she have before they came in?

Soundlessly she tiptoed across the room to a cupboard in the far corner. There should be a vial inside, but when her fingers gently pulled the drawer open and she looked down her heart sank. The drawer was completely empty. There was only one other place in the house that she knew there was *definitely* a vial to create a pathway. It was upstairs in the desk in her own room. Could she get up there without being seen? Her heart was now hammering so loudly in her chest that she feared the pulver would hear it. Taking a deep breath she made her way towards the door.

'She's not here,' one of the guards was saying.

'Harrow's a fool if he thinks she would come back home,' a second one added.

'Yeah, as if she would do *that* knowing that all of us are out looking for her,' said a third.

'Strange though,' the first one replied. I'd never have believed that the Lady Yelenia would have turned traitor and gone over to the other side.'

'Yes, Parenon himself always had such a high regard

for her. I wonder if he has been told of her treachery?'

Helen's head spun. Not only had Harrow told them that she was a traitor – but they had all believed him! It made her want to sob with the injustice of it all.

There was no time for self pity though. The next words of the pulver guard outside the door gave her a brief moment of hope.

'Pointless us staying here anyway, we've searched all the rooms.'

She gave a huge sigh of relief. 'They must already have looked in this room before I even got here!' she thought. 'That means they won't come back in here. A stroke of luck at long last!'

After a few grunts and words of agreement from the other guards, Helen heard them begin to make their way to the front door. She strained her ears for the sound of the door closing behind them. When she was certain that the hallway was empty she carefully opened the door.

The way upstairs was clear. The pulver had gone. Forgetting the ache in her arm from where she had fallen on it Helen ran towards the bottom of the staircase. She grabbed hold of the newel post at the bottom of the banister and used it to swing herself around quickly onto the bottom steps. She raced upwards.

But even before she was halfway up the staircase the front door opened again behind her!

'...sure I just left it here behind the d... Hey!' the returning pulver shouted. 'Stop right there!'

Stopping was the last thing that Helen was going to do. She hurled herself up the remaining stairs two at a time and hurtled down the upstairs corridor to her room.

The pulver was already on the stairs. His training made him as swift as a hunting pedjiaar. He was gaining on her by the second.

Helen threw herself through her bedroom door and made straight to the desk in the corner. This was where she kept her trinkets and valuables, as well as her secret vial and the kron. The drawers of the desk were open, and many of her things had been strewn around the room.

The pulver guards had been thorough, but not thorough enough. Helen slid the heavy desk sideways and round into the middle of the room. At the back, on one of the panels that held the desk together, there was a tiny hole. The hole was just big enough for Helen to get her little finger through. She wriggled it around inside the panel of wood until there was a dull click. She grinned as a strip of wood came away easily in her hand revealing a secret compartment.

This private drawer contained the vial and her kron. She knew that it was too late to attempt to sidestep on her own; she had been perfecting the skill recently but it would still take too much energy and time. The footsteps were getting closer outside. She put the kron in her pocket and reached instead for the vial sitting next to it. It was tucked away right at the back of the little secret drawer. Her fingers closed over it eagerly as she heard the pulver race through the door behind her.

'Stop! Don't move! That's an order!'

Her hand swept across her desk, scrabbling for something, anything to take her away from this danger.

So many things had been disturbed by the pulver's searching that Helen did not know what she might find. She clutched at the first object she came to. In an instant, before she even looked down to see what this thing was, and before the guard could stop her, Helen had tipped the contents of the vial over the object. She felt the low murmur begin as a pathway began to open. A column of white light sprang up around her as Harrow also dashed in. He raised his arms towards her desperately but he was too late to stop her disappearing through the pathway.

She felt the familiar sickening motion of being sucked upwards through the swirling column of light. But what was it that she had picked up from her desk? And where was the pathway taking her?

Riding up Roseberry

Helen was being pulled upwards through the pathway. Her body twisted around like a corkscrew as she hurtled through the tunnel of pure energy.

Her hand was still clenched tightly around the object that she had picked up from her desk as the pulver had rushed into the room. She couldn't look down to see what it was because her head was being forced upwards as she tore along the pathway. Instead she ran her fingers over the surface. It was a flat, circular shape made of smooth, silky fabric. The fabric felt as if it had been folded repeatedly around what seemed to be a cardboard circle in the middle. There was a small, cold piece of metal fastened to the back of the card.

Immediately, Helen realised what the object in her hand was. One of her prize rosettes for horse riding and show jumping!

When she was younger she had visited the local stables near to their home in Darlington on Earth. She had won four or five rosettes at events held by the stable's owner. Now she knew where the pathway would take her!

The sickening, spinning sensation began to slow down. Helen's eyes were clenched shut. This was the part of travelling the pathways that she hated most – the landing!

She felt the ground under her feet and threw out her

arms to steady her balance. When she opened her eyes the bright white light around her had already begun to grow dimmer and was turning to a pinkish hue. A fierce heat came up from the ground under the soles of her feet and she stepped out of the light.

Helen looked around her. She was standing in a muddy yard covered with puddles. It had obviously been raining heavily quite recently.

Nearby on her right was a pile of straw bales. They were stacked five high and towered over her. Next to them was a long old rusty trough, half filled with water. Across the yard, some fifty metres away, was a row of stables. Two or three upper doors were open and horses peered out inquisitively at her. She thought she even recognised one of them.

It was the smell in her nostrils that reminded her of this place more strongly than anything else, however. It was a warm and pungent reek of manure that wrinkled your nose at first, yet felt comforting at the same time.

Helen knew that she didn't have long. Harrow might follow her at any moment. He only had to pick up an object belonging to her, a scrap of clothing, even something that she had recently held in her hand. With his skills that would be enough for him to create a pathway straight to her.

She looked around hurriedly. The stables were not far from the base of a range of hills. The nearest of these was called Roseberry Topping. It was a couple of miles away from the village where she lived with her parents when they were on Earth. Two miles was too far to run through open countryside with the possibility of someone stronger and faster chasing her. She could saddle up a horse and *ride* there though!

But even as she began to run towards the stables she

realised that going straight home was probably not the best idea. She would be followed home for sure! That was the most obvious place to look for her as soon as it was realised that she had come to Earth.

As she paused in indecision, a figure stepped through one of the stable doors. It was a girl of about her own age and she was leading a chestnut coloured mare on a halter. Helen recognised her immediately. It was Megan, one of the daughters of Mr. Thomas who owned the stables.

Megan saw Helen in the same instant. She looked surprised, then puzzled, but then her face broke into a delighted grin.

'Helen! Helen Day!'

'Hi there,' Helen replied. She tried to sound as normal as she could, although her head was still spinning after the journey.

'I haven't seen you for a while. Dad didn't say that you had booked a lesson.'

'It's a bit of a sudden decision.'

'Good to see you again, Mel and I have missed you. You've not been around here for ages.' Mel was Megan's sister.

'No,' Helen was thinking rapidly. 'We've been away staying with my relatives in London.'

This was believable enough, she thought. She was sure that she had mentioned the fact that she had an aunt, uncle and cousin in London a few years ago. Harrow had taught her that if she did have to deceive others to get herself out of trouble, it was best to include as much truth within the lie as you could. Not only will it be more believable, he had said, but it will also be easier for you to remember what you have said. (Now she knew just how good at lying he really was.)

In any case, Megan seemed to accept her explanation

without further questions.

'It would be great to get out riding with you again after all this time,' she said.

'That would be fun,' Helen replied. She glanced around her nervously. 'But I was hoping to get out pretty much straight away.'

'Well, I know there are a couple of horses free at the moment, and Jigsaw is already saddled,' her old friend continued. 'Give me five minutes and I'll get a saddle and reins on Zarak as well.'

Helen nodded agreement. Even in the midst of her fear and anxiety it would be good to have the company.

'Where is Jigsaw?' she asked. 'I'll go and introduce myself to him again. I wonder if he'll recognise me after all this time.'

'Follow me. He's over here.'

Megan began to lead Helen towards the far end of the stables.

Before they reached it, Helen heard a familiar whinny. The docile, friendly face of Jigsaw, her favourite pony, peered out and nodded at her over the half door of the stable. Even after two years it seemed that he did still recognise her. She grinned back at him.

'Hello beautiful. How are you?'

Jigsaw snickered at her, showing his teeth in his own wide grin. He nodded his head again, more vigorously this time, shaking the bridle on his head so that it rattled. It was easy to see why he was called Jigsaw. His coat was a patchwork of pale chocolate brown and white irregular markings. They seemed to fit together like the large pieces of a puzzle. Just seeing him again lifted Helen's heart in spite of the secrets she had recently discovered and the dangers she knew might come racing after her through a pathway at any time.

'Lead him out and mount up,' Megan instructed her. 'I'll bring Zarak out.'

'Will do.'

Helen nuzzled Jigsaw as she opened the bolt of the door and swung it outwards. The warm smell of the pony was like a blanket to comfort her.

'Good boy. You won't let anyone catch me will you?'

She spoke softly as she put her left foot into the stirrup. Grabbing the pommel of the saddle she began to swing herself up onto the pony's back. She had taken too long already. Much as she would have liked to wait for Megan, she knew she had to get away from the stables.

There was a wide, gravelled footpath winding around the bottom of the hill. Above her, Roseberry Topping climbed up into a pale grey sky. She urged Jigsaw into a canter. He kicked up his hooves happily and sped forwards so that Helen had to lean over his neck, rising up out of the saddle. Her riding skills came back to her immediately, and she made subtle adjustments in her balance, gripping the pony with her legs as he accelerated even more into a fast gallop.

The wind whistled in her ears and whipped her hair around her face, blocking her vision for a moment. With both hands on the reins she had to shake her head to see clearly.

As she did so, she felt Jigsaw suddenly falter. His easy, galloping strides broke their rhythm and he twisted sideways, whinnying in surprise and fear. Helen had to grasp the pommel of the saddle to stop herself from falling off. What had startled Jigsaw so much? She wondered fearfully.

All of a sudden her hair blew back from her face again. A white column of light had appeared only ten metres in front of them. Over the noise of the wind in her ears Helen could now hear the easily recognisable humming sound of a pathway opening up. The light was already dimming and turning to a deep blood-red. Helen could make out the outline of a familiar figure in its midst; a tall figure in a long black cloak with a thick, bushy beard.

'Harrow!' she cursed under her breath.

Digging her heels in Jigsaw's ribs, she pulled heavily on the right hand rein. The pony turned as she wanted and began to race up the steep scree-covered slope of the hillside.

Helen dare not look behind her. Panic drove her on. Jigsaw was valiantly scrambling upwards, but his hooves scrabbled and slipped dangerously on the stones and scree.

'Come on my beauty!' Helen whispered, her head low down over his neck and her lips close to his ears.

'Yelenia!' Harrow's voice behind her was harsh and urgent. She ignored it and kicked Jigsaw into an upwards canter once more.

'I'll not warn you again!' he shouted.

'Then save your breath, you traitor!' she grunted to herself under her breath. 'I'll never listen to you again anyway.' She had seen the tell tale flicker of light around Harrow's fingers.

Tears began to run down her cheeks. She wasn't sure if they were caused by the sorrow of betrayal, fear, or the wind that had turned suddenly cold and stung her eyes.

She could see, not far above them, a level stretch of ground where one of the footpaths leading to the summit of Roseberry curled back on itself around the side of the hill. They were almost there. If she could just get Jigsaw onto that level path then she knew they could speed away far enough from Harrow for a few moments. That might just give her a chance to dismount and create another pathway.

Behind her, Cleve Harrow was summoning all his

power. He could not let the Lady Yelenia escape again. There was simply too much at stake. She was destined to be an unfortunate sacrifice for the greater, long-lasting good of all the people of Beltheron and Earth. If she escaped, she might do as she had threatened and tell Serrion the full extent of all the secrets and lies that entangled him.

If that happened, Harrow knew that Serrion would never agree to play the part that had been prepared for him. The part that was so vital in the final destruction of the evil agents of Atros.

Tears now appeared in Harrow's eyes also. Tears of frustration, despair and deep, deep regret. How had everything gone so wrong? But he knew he had no choice. He knew what he had to do now.

With a cry of anguish, Cleve Harrow pointed his hand towards his target and a blaze of light shot towards Helen and her pony...

Destiny in the Great Hall

The noise was deafening. War cries and screams of pain jarred with the cawing of angry birds and the whinnying of horse and holva. Orianna felt numbed by the clamour surrounding her as she clung to Parenon's arm.

They ran along the side streets towards Ungolin's palace. Parenon knew that the captains organising the pulver forces would rally there and use it as a base for operations in the war with the rish.

It was difficult to stay hidden. The two of them kept ducking into the shadows and doorways, but it seemed that the birds were everywhere. Parenon covered both of them with his cloak as best he could, but both were cut and bruised by the beaks and small bodies that hurled themselves at the pair of them in fury. Orianna wondered at the blind, senseless rage that was driving the birds. Such rage terrified her. It had no logic, no reasoning behind it.

At last they reached the wide steps that led up to Ungolin's palace.

They paused in the shadows. The birds were still in a frenzy above them.

Then, hope arrived in the shape of a large group of men who suddenly turned a corner, running towards them so swiftly that they almost knocked Orianna and Parenon off their feet. There were over fifty of them, Parenon guessed. These men were not in the regulation uniform and pale blue cloaks of the pulver, but were more of a rag-tag bunch of brigands. They were rebels and Parenon immediately recognised the leader.

'Tarawen!'

'Captain!' he replied in surprise. 'I have travelled from Atros with my men, but I fear I am too late. What in the Three Worlds has happened to these birds?'

'No time to explain,' Parenon yelled at him, 'you must get us into Ungolin's Hall.'

With a few brief instructions to his men, Tarawen arranged them into groups. They spread out over the steps and into the square, firing arrows and hurling spears up into the flocks of birds. As they drew their attention away, Tarawen and Parenon leapt up to the doors, closely followed by Orianna. In a flurry of swinging and stabbing blades the two men swiftly dispatched the rish guards at the doorways and the three sped in.

Tarawen paused and looked back towards his rebels who were still battling the birds outside. More rish were now running into the square.

'Go to your men,' Parenon ordered. 'They need you.'

'But sir,'

'No time to argue, go now. We will be fine.'

Tarawen turned and sped back down the steps outside as Orianna took Parenon's hand.

They ran inside Ungolin's palace together and raced towards the great hall.

Moments later, out in the square, a low humming sound began and a tall column of light appeared. Tarawen paused in his tracks to watch. With a sigh of relief he recognised Serrion appear as the light of the pathway dimmed around them.

He did not waste a moment and ran across the square. 'Serrion! Over here!'

The rebel waved and grabbing Serrion's arm he pulled him through the melee of fighting rebels, rish and birds. Serrion allowed himself to be led through the crowds. His face was blank, and in spite of all the turmoil around him the only thing he could think of was the final sight of Vishan and Sophia disappearing in the flash of light under the waters of the river.

In a hurried conversation, Tarawen informed him of the state of the battle. At the mention of Orianna, Serrion stiffened and suddenly broke out of his memories.

'My sister!' he yelled as he grabbed at Tarawen's sleeve. 'Where is she?'

'Parenon has taken her into the great hall,' Tarawen replied.

Without a moment's hesitation, Serrion sprinted from the rebel leader and towards the steps of Ungolin's palace.

Parenon and Orianna rounded a corner at the end of a tapestried corridor. Standing directly in front of them, half way up the final set of steps that led to the great hall itself, was Piotre Andresen. His hard eyes shone brightly in his cruel face. He held the golden staff of Beltheron in his hands.

Parenon stopped in his tracks and with a swift movement, pushed Orianna behind him so he stood between her and the Lord of Atros.

Piotre looked at both of them for a moment. Then, with realisation in his eyes he began to grin.

'Oh, perfect!' he laughed. 'How sweet! The two of you are in love! That makes my job now so much easier.'

He aimed the golden staff directly at Parenon.

'Keep behind me!' Parenon yelled at Orianna.

Light flashed from the golden staff towards him. Parenon parried the fiery blast with his sword, but the blow was so strong that it almost knocked him off his feet. He ran forwards up the wide steps, directly towards Piotre. Piotre just laughed again, but the pulver was remarkably quick. In a moment he was at Piotre's side, swinging his blade again. Metal and gold met with a ringing clash that reverberated around the room. Sparks, both real and magical, showered around them on each impact as they fought so that it looked as if they were surrounded by fireworks.

Orianna watched, both fascinated and fearful, as the two men circled each other. They moved so swiftly that their cloaks billowed about them like blue and black banners in a high wind. It was hard to tell which one had the upper hand as they struggled up and down the steps. She was trying to find a moment when she could intervene, to try to help Parenon, but the two men were so close together she could not find the chance.

Parenon was the younger and faster of the two, but Piotre had the extra power of the staff on his side. Each blow weakened Parenon as if he had been struck several times. It was not long before Orianna realised he could not defeat the Lord of Atros alone. She had to do something quickly!

Orianna struggled deep into her memory and then reached forward with both hands, she began to intone one of her old spells.

'*Aurelior posito reversium!*' nothing happened at first. She repeated the words again. '*Aurelior posito reversium!*' Orianna had never concentrated so hard on anything before. All the anger and sorrow she felt about what had happened to her mother, all the love she shared with

Parenon and her hopes for the two of them, and her sense of duty towards her brother and Beltheron were now bound up in a potent intention. Focusing all of this onto Piotre Andresen, she spoke the words for a third time.

'*Aurelior posito reversium!*'

This time the golden staff began to tremble in Piotre's hands. His expression changed from one of exultant victory, to bemusement and fear. With a cry of shock he suddenly dropped the staff as if it had become too hot to hold.

As soon as it was released, the golden staff shot towards Orianna's outstretched hands.

Piotre turned towards her furiously then sped up the steps before Parenon could raise his sword for the final blow. He disappeared through the shattered doorway and out of sight into the great hall.

Parenon sped after him. This new turn of events had given him a fresh hope and renewed energy. With his favourite battle cry of 'For Mage and Council!' he leapt into the hall after his enemy.

Orianna raced up the steps in pursuit, still holding onto the golden staff.

His voice rang out again, 'For Orianna!' as she ran into the room. Parenon's sword was above Piotre's head and he was about to deliver the final blow.

But even as he did there was a strangled cry of '*Father!*' from the corner of the room behind them. Orianna turned and saw Jacques point the black staff of Atros towards Piotre.

In front of their eyes, Piotre vanished in a blaze of pure, white light. As he did the power of the magic that Jacques had released shattered all the windows of the hall. Parenon staggered backwards with the blast. He had come so close to killing Piotre Andresen! Now Jacques had removed his father from danger and Parenon had been robbed of his victory at the very last moment.

Without a word, Jacques stepped forwards. He swung the black staff in Orianna's direction and she felt a sudden heavy blow to her side. She crumpled to the ground in agony, letting go of the golden staff as she clutched at her stomach. Her head struck the cold stone of the floor.

Jacques laughed in triumph and reached into his robes to draw his sword.

The last thing Orianna was aware of as she faded out of consciousness was Parenon running towards her, his arm raised to protect her, and Jacques stepping in to slice at the pulver's body with a long gleaming blade...

Harrow's Fall

Megan had taken longer than usual to get the saddle onto Zarak's back. For some reason he was in a strange mood today. He normally loved the chance to get out into the hills for a gallop, especially after the rain when the air up on the Cleveland Hills seemed fresh and new.

But today he dug in his hooves and it took all her efforts and cajoling to get him to even step out of the stable.

'What is it, boy?' she asked.

He snickered and whinnied in reply. His eyes rolled as if in fear. Megan wondered what it was that was disturbing him. He was usually so easy to get along with.

'Don't be so silly! There's nothing to worry about. We're going to go for a lovely long ride with Helen and Jigsaw up onto the tops. You like that, don't you?'

Eventually the horse gave in. Megan led him out into the yard. He was a gorgeous creature, a deep ochre colour that shimmered and gleamed as he moved forwards and his muscles rippled.

They rode quickly up the side of the hill. Megan was surprised that Helen had already managed to get so far. Even as she rounded a bend on Zarak, and reached the part of the path that began to wind more steeply, she still could not see her up ahead.

'Maybe I made a mistake,' Megan thought to herself. 'Perhaps Helen didn't come this way after all.' She looked around her as she rode, searching for her old friend.

She thought that she would just carry on a little bit further. If she could not see Helen after another minute of riding then she would head back and look for her along one of the other tracks.

'Silly girl,' she thought. 'What was the rush about? After nearly two years, couldn't she just wait for me at the bottom for another five minutes?'

Just then she saw a strange flash of light in the air not far off.

It was up ahead of her, in the direction that she had been riding. Zarak whinnied again, and hopped nervously, trying to turn himself and Megan around. But she was having none of it.

'Sorry boy, but this is just too strange,' she encouraged him with her calmest voice. 'You and I are going to investigate.'

She spurred him on faster up the hill until he was going at a steady canter. Then she heard the voices. One was Helen's – she was sure of it – but the other one she didn't recognise at all. One thing that was clear to her though, there was a serious argument going on. Even though she couldn't make out all of the words, the angry tone in the man's voice was unmistakeable.

Megan rounded another corner and there in front of her was the most bizarre thing she had ever seen.

Only a hundred metres away, Helen could be seen on Jigsaw, who was rearing up on his hind legs in fear. In front of them stood a strangely dressed man with his back to Megan. He was dressed in a long black coat that hung down around him like a cloak. The strangest thing of all was the light which had begun to glow around the ends of his fingers. He seemed to be pointing his hands towards Helen, and the terror on her face was clear to Megan, even from this distance.

Without another moment's thought she spurred Zarak into a gallop. She got closer, and saw the light flare more brightly from the stranger's hands.

Over the thundering of Zarak's hooves she heard him say: 'I'll not warn you again!' and in the distance Helen muttered a reply that Megan could not make out.

Then several things happened at once. A ball of fire shot from the bearded stranger's hands as Zarak hit him squarely in the back at full tilt. Megan was thrown out of the saddle and onto the ground with the violence of the impact.

The cloaked stranger gave an anguished cry of pain, shock, and fury as he was hurled over the edge of the path and down the steep slope of Roseberry... The ball of light that he had fired at Helen zoomed into the air and exploded harmlessly several metres above their heads.

Harrow continued rolling head over heels down the slope and then, with a cry of alarm, he fell away out of sight over a ridge.

Megan struggled to get back onto her feet. She still held onto the reins which were tangled around Zarak's neck. Thankfully he quickly recovered from the events of the last few moments, and soon stood placidly so that Megan could recover from her fall.

Her head spun and, as her vision slowly cleared she saw Helen looking down at her with concern.

'Megan? Megan! Are you alright?'

She shook her head to clear it.

'I think so, thanks,' she replied.

'No, thank *you*! I don't know what I would have done if you hadn't come up just then.'

'Who was that?'

'No time to explain,' Helen was peering over the

edge where Harrow had disappeared moments before. It was a long drop down and she couldn't make out any sign of the Cleve. She shuddered. Half of her was relieved, but the other half was terrified. Had Megan just killed Cleve Harrow?

Megan was still gazing at her questioningly. Helen realised that she must pull herself together.

'All you need to know is that that man down there is very dangerous and you did an extremely brave thing just now,' Helen considered for a second. 'Trouble is, if he *does* come back up he's going to be very angry with you.'

'I don't like the sound of that, but we'll just ride back down to the stables and I'll get my dad to...'

'Sorry, Megan, but that's not going to be enough. Oh dear, I really didn't mean to involve you in all this.'

Megan looked at her as if her friend had suddenly lost her wits.

'All what? Come on Helen, you're not making any sense. We've known each other long enough, haven't we? Tell me what's going on!'

Helen thought for a long moment. Where could she begin? And even if she did tell Megan the truth, it was so fantastical that she would never believe her. Yet she knew that she couldn't just leave her here. She had seen Harrow's fury and – if he *had* survived that fall – she had no idea what he might do in retribution. She had to get Megan to safety. Helen took a deep breath.

'It is really complicated, Megan,' she began. 'The best way is if I just show you.'

'That's fine with me.'

'Megan, this will be difficult for you to understand.'

'That's ok. I just want to know what's going on, Helen.'

Helen nodded. 'Fair enough. Do you trust me?'

'Trust you? Of course I trust you.'

'We'll have to leave the horses here for now. They won't like what I'm about to do.'

They stepped away from the horses and walked a little way down the slope. They paused and Helen looked all around her to make sure they were alone.

Megan stared as Helen took a rosette and a small vial out of her pocket and began to unscrew the lid. She tilted it and let a few drops fall onto the rosette between her fingers.

'Hold on tightly to my waist,' Helen said. 'I'm taking you back to the stables.'

'What do you mean? Why don't we ride?'

'This is much quicker.'

'But what about the horses?'

'You can come and pick them up later, when it's safe. Trust me, Megan. Just do as I say and hold on tight.'

Megan threw her arms around her friend as a column of light began to shine around them. Her screams of surprise and terror were hidden by the throbbing sound that filled the air as they disappeared through the pathway.

Helen dropped Megan off at the stables. She tried her best to convince the poor girl not to speak about the things that she had seen. Megan was looking so shocked and disbelieving about what had just happened that Helen thought she probably wouldn't want to tell anybody about it anyway. Then Helen made her way back to her own house and safety. She needed to find things there that would allow her to create another pathway. She had to get back to Beltheron, she realised. Her work was not finished yet.

Revenge at last

Orianna's head was spinning. She was crumpled on the cold tiles on the floor of the great hall. Her long white hair was streaked with red as blood seeped from the deep wound above her ear. She felt sick. How had this happened? How had everything turned so dreadfully wrong?

She heard a voice inside her head. It was cruel and teasing, saying something about revenge and justice. She thought that she recognised the voice. Was it a memory of someone she had once known? Then she realised that it wasn't in her head at all; the person speaking was in the great hall with her. She lifted her head and slowly focused on the figure in front of her.

Jacques Andresen stood there gloating. A wicked leer spread across his lips. At his feet was the crumpled body of her beloved Parenon, his pale blue cloak tangled and soaking up the dark pool that spread around him on the floor. His right arm had been flung out in his final moments, to try to reach the golden staff that still lay on the ground just beyond his reach. She let out a sob.

Jacques stood over the body of the dead pulver. He gave it a dismissive kick and stepped towards her. In his right hand was the long black staff of Atros. Crimson flame flickered at its tip. His left hand held a long sword that was pointing to her throat.

'Welcome back Dove Hair,' he sneered. 'I thought that

you were already dead after that blow I gave you. But it seems you are stronger than your brave, stupid captain here. That is good, because I want to have a little more fun with you first before I do kill you.' His eyes were filled with a manic glee.

Orianna choked back the sickness of terror and grief that she felt rising up in her throat. He was quite, quite mad, she realised. There could be no talking, no reasoning with him.

Jacques was raising the black staff over his head. Its obsidian darkness seemed to spread out through the room, and pressed oppressively against Orianna's temples. The sword in his other hand began to make small circles in the air close to her throat, taunting her, terrifying her. He grinned down again and moved the tip of the sword until it hovered over her face, tracing little lines over her cheek.

Orianna closed her eyes. 'Please,' she thought to herself as she felt the pressure of the blade grow heavier. 'Please just make it quick.'

Suddenly a voice rang out from across the hall.

'Don't you dare touch her!'

Jacques spun around. There, at the broken entrance to the hall, stood Serrion. The wind whipped through the shattered windows, flicking his long black and white hair around his face. His eyes filled with fury and hatred as he began to descend the stairs towards his enemy.

'A warning?' taunted Jacques. He still stood motionless above Orianna, with his sword centimetres from her left eye. 'You give me a warning by getting me to turn around instead of just killing me from behind?' he laughed scornfully. 'Have you learnt nothing from your training with those ridiculous pulver?'

'Shut up!' yelled Serrion. 'Just shut up and move away from her!'

Jacques remained where he was and laughed again. Serrion yelled even louder.

'I warn you, if you even *touch* my sister I'll … I'll…' Serrion's words failed him in his rage and anxiety for Orianna. He had seen Parenon's poor body on the ground, and this too filled him with fear. If Jacques could defeat even Parenon, then what hope did *he* have?

'Just… just move away from her,' he ended, lamely.

"Move away? Oh I think not,' Jacques replied, still circling the tip of his blade so dangerously, terrifyingly close to Orianna's face. 'You are the one who needs to move away, or it will be the worse for *her!*'

As he spat out the final word his sword jabbed towards Orianna's cheek, piercing it so that a trickle of blood began to run down her face. She winced and cried out.

Serrion's mouth grew very thin as he clenched his lips together in frustration. He had never felt so angry – or so powerless. Tears sprang to his eyes but he shook them away. What could he do? One move from him and Jacques's sword would plunge into Orianna's prone body. His eyes flickered this way and that, looking for anything that might help him; anything that might give him an advantage, or an idea. Jacques was standing in the middle of the vast hall. There was no way to get to him without endangering Orianna even more.

There was nothing Serrion could use nearby to distract Jacques' attention. The golden staff lay on the floor but that was too far away to reach, and he would have to leap over Parenon's body to get to it. There was nothing else to aid him.

Nothing at all … except Jacques' own pride.

Yes, thought Serrion. That was it. That was the only weapon that he had against the taunting, arrogant young man in front of him. His own sense of invulnerability, his own sense of pride. That was the only weapon that he could now turn against his enemy.

Serrion thought rapidly. How to do it? He would have to judge his performance perfectly in the next few moments so as to trick Jacques and not have him suspect anything. No time to think it through, Serrion decided. He just had to go for it.

He let his shoulders drop down and his sword hung loosely at his side. His head drooped and he gave a sigh.

'Alright, Jacques. You win.'

Jacques' face lit up with glee.

'Hah, say it again, gutter boy! I didn't hear you.'

'You hold all the advantages, so you win. You are quicker than me, and stronger. You have Orianna. So, I give in. Just let her go. Please?'

As Serrion said these words he had begun to walk slowly and dejectedly down the staircase. His arms still hung limply by his sides. He even let his sword drag on the steps, clanging on the stone of each one as he descended. He did not look as if he was posing any threat at all to the other boy.

Jacques had brought his own sword up fractionally. It was no longer aimed in Orianna's direction. She had noticed this and was watching her brother intently, every fibre of her being tensed and ready to move, watching for what he was about to do.

Jacques even took a step or two away from her as Serrion reached the bottom of the staircase. Jacques stood up to his full height, preening himself arrogantly.

'Maybe,' thought Serrion to himself, 'just maybe this is working!'

'So you admit it,' Jacques sneered. 'I am the stronger one. At last you realise that you could never win. No, not against me and my family. We are the Beltheron Select, rightful leaders and powerful beyond your dreams. So now, get on your knees in front of me, down on the ground where you belong, gutter boy!'

Serrion took another few paces forwards. He was almost close enough to Jacques to strike out at him. Yet even now he waited to make his move, for Jacques still held both the sword and the black staff aloft. Serrion knew that he was still at a disadvantage. He had to catch the other boy completely off his guard.

'On your knees I said!' Jacques repeated. "Bow down before me!'

Serrion sank down to his knees. In the corner of his eye he saw his sister slowly and silently begin to get to her feet.

He held out his sword in both hands, offering it up towards Jacques.

'Here, take it,' he began. 'Like I say, you win. You are the strongest.'

Jacques began to leer at him. His mouth grew wider and wider into a crazy grin. He stepped forward. As he did he sheathed his own sword and held out his free hand to take the one proffered by Serrion.

Still kneeling, Serrion spun his blade back into his right hand then swung it in a fast, wide arc. It sliced into Jacques' forearm, making him scream in pain and anger.

Serrion had leapt up instantly and was on his feet already, swinging the sword a second time. Jacques was still in such shock from the pain that he was caught off guard, gazing disbelievingly at the blood trickling from the wound in his arm, as if frozen to the spot.

The second blow of Serrion's blade made direct contact with the black staff of Atros. But this was Serrion's mistake, for as the two connected there was a loud, ringing clang. It was like the sound of a mighty brass gong being struck by a metal hammer. The crimson fire at the tip of the staff exploded into a vivid palette of reds, oranges and yellowy golden colours that filled the room. All three of them were blinded for a couple of seconds.

At the moment of impact with the black staff, Serrion's sword shattered into a thousand fragments. He staggered backwards, jolted by the blow, his hand trembling and suddenly red hot. Jacques laughed manically.

'And yet again you make a simple mistake!' Now feel the true power of the black staff of Atros!'

He raised the dark staff over his head, rippling flame now running up and down its entire length. A bolt of dark fire shot out and struck Serrion in the chest hurling him backwards.

Jacques suddenly became aware of another movement behind him. He turned in his moment of victory to see Orianna running towards him. She had picked up the golden staff of Beltheron and now held it in both hands, high over her head. He raised the black staff to meet it and as those two symbols of power and ancient magic struck each other there was a huge explosion. The remaining windows shattered and the very foundations of the great hall were shaken. Ungolin's throne trembled on its ancient dais.

Orianna and Jacques remained standing in the midst of the noise and turmoil, the power in the weapons they held making them proof against the violence and noise that surrounded them. The two staves were melded together at their tip, crackling and shimmering, while each of them tried to force the other backwards. The blonde boy and the white haired young woman were locked together in fury, neither willing to surrender their hold.

Jacques' eyes held hers, and he grunted between clenched teeth. 'Let it go, Dove Hair. Your mother died releasing a great evil into the world that you wished to protect. Your brother and lover are also dead or dying. What is left for you now? Nothing but shame for your mother's actions and pain for the memory of your lost loved ones. Let it go and give in. Give in to me! The new young Lord of Atros!'

Orianna closed her eyes. It seemed to Jacques that she was indeed about to give in to him. Now, finally, he believed that he had won after all. His eyes glittered with evil excitement.

But Orianna did not let go of the golden staff. She did not give in. Under her breath she began to speak those words she had recently memorised.

'*Imperilar rabensmancer landeyeda! Toto derelictum in scrupulor mantasis!*'

Her voice rose to a scream on the last word of the incantation. Her pure white hair flowed around her head. She opened her eyes again and now a fierce light shone in them. A huge jolt of energy swept through Orianna's body and along the length of the golden staff. With a mighty boom that threw all of them across the room, the black staff of Atros exploded. Pieces of dark shrapnel hurtled through the air in all directions, whistling terrifyingly close to their heads, embedding themselves in the stonework and shredding tapestries in their flight.

There was a momentary silence in the room. Serrion shook his head to clear it. He looked around. As his vision cleared he saw Orianna. She had been thrown to the ground but was already beginning to sit up. She didn't seem to be too seriously injured. Then he saw Jacques, struggling to his knees. He was looking around urgently for a weapon.

Serrion cast his eyes around hurriedly. Without his sword he had no way to fight. He spotted a couple of long, dark shapes on the floor nearby, the fragments of the sundered black staff. Serrion hurled himself towards the largest one. He raised it high in his fist and ran towards Jacques.

The young Andresen was still staggering to his feet from where he had been thrown by the force of Orianna's incantation. Serrion did not pause however. There was no pity left in him as once there might have been; nothing now to stay his hand. He leapt upon his enemy with a triumphant shout.

He aimed directly at Jacques's heart, but mis-timed his blow in his fury. The point of the broken shard of the black staff went wide of its mark and plunged into Jacques' shoulder. As it did he heard Orianna cry out.

'Serrion! Behind you! Look out!'

In the same instant that his sister called the warning he heard the heavy flap of wings. His heart turned cold in his breast. He twisted around to see the bird-form of Larena swooping down towards him from high in the hall. Her beak was wide open and her sharp talons spread in front of her, ready for attack. He had only a second before she struck.

Still holding onto the other end of the piece of broken staff, Serrion spun around, twisting Jacques with him. The young Lord of Atros gave a cry of agony as the shards of obsidian ground around deeper in his shoulder. He turned with Serrion as they both came around to face the plunging raven. Jacques had no choice but to turn in the direction that Serrion moved him, it was the only way to prevent the staff from piercing his shoulder even deeper.

As they both turned together in this kind of bizarre dance, Larena's dive faltered. Her prey had moved so quickly! In the last instant she tried to alter the course of her flight, but had been so intent on violent retribution that she could not stop herself. Her talons missed Serrion and raked across Jacques' face instead as he was spun into her path.

The force knocked Jacques to the ground. With a groan Serrion was hurled across the room. The broken piece of the black staff was wrenched from Jacques' shoulder and clattered across the stone floor out of reach of any of them. Serrion rolled away behind a large oak chair lying on its side by one of the tables.

Larena was already in the air again, wings flapping frantically, cawing in anger as she looked this way and that for Serrion.

Meanwhile, Orianna had struggled to her feet. The sword that Jacques had dropped during his struggle was only a metre away. She dived headlong towards it, ignoring the pounding pain in her temples as Larena readied herself to strike again.

Orianna sensed the terrifying shadow passing over her head and dropped to the ground, her arm reaching for the blade. Larena missed her by centimetres, screeching in frustration a second time, and rose again into the air.

A flash of memory of her mother and beloved Parenon spurred Orianna on and in one movement she had rolled over, picking up the handle of the sword. As she turned onto her back, Larena's shadow still above her, she hurled it straight up into the air in the same instant as Larena dived for the third time.

The sword pierced the Birdwoman's breast – the force and speed of her own dive plunging it deep into her heart. Her raven's head was flung backwards in shock and sudden pain. The tiny bright black eyes widened and looked almost human for a brief moment. Larena was suspended motionless in the air for what seemed like whole seconds, as if time itself were slowing down to a standstill. Then the huge bird began to fall. Its wings folded and crumpled as the body tumbled towards the ground.

Orianna was still directly underneath. Even though

she felt numb with the pain and exertion she had enough of her wits about her to realise she was still in mortal danger. Larena was about to fall on top of her! With what seemed like the very last of her strength, Orianna rolled away once more to try to get out of her path.

But even as the corpse of the Birdwoman fell, it changed. Tiny sparks began to illuminate her outline. She shrank quickly as she fell and became less solid. With just a few centimetres left before she hit Orianna, there was a breath of air and nothing more than a cascade of dark feathers fluttered down on top of her.

Serrion sensed all this happening over to his left, but his attention was still mainly focused on Jacques. He had to keep the upper hand! He would not, *could* not be defeated! Not now, not after all the things that he had been through, everything that he had learnt about himself. In the last two years he had faced danger, betrayal and hatred. But he had also met with love, loyalty and affection, and it was the first time in his life that he had truly experienced them. It was these things which gave him strength now. The death and the danger had certainly changed him – made him colder, self reliant and more resilient to hardship – but the love and loyalty had made him stronger in other ways and had helped him to grow. He had a different strength now. Not just physical strength from his training with the pulver, but a strength of character, and a deeper understanding of things that were worth fighting for and preserving. Having lost so much he now valued even more the few things that were left to him.

He noticed that Jacques had risen to his feet. A cry of anguish formed on his lips as he saw what had happened to Larena. The anguish turned to rage and he ran towards Orianna once more. Serrion hauled himself to his feet from behind the chair where he had been flung. Ignoring the pain he felt through his whole body he threw himself at Jacques before he had time to reach Orianna. He hit his adversary full on in the chest. The breath was forced from both their bodies with the impact and they crashed onto the floor, locked together in a fury of flailing fists and biting teeth. There were no rules left, no Pulver training, no strategy. This was a dirty, frantic brawl to the finish.

Over and over on the ground they rolled, punching and kicking, each one trying to get a stronger hold on the other. Their pummelling became more frantic. Staggering to their feet, Jacques managed to get his hands around Serrion's throat and had begun to squeeze. Serrion pushed backwards towards the wall, forcing Jacques heavily against a torn tapestry. As his body hit the wall hard, Jacques gave a gasp. His eyes went very wide and his grip around Serrion's throat slackened. Jacques made a strange gurgling sound and his whole body went limp. His blond head slumped forwards onto his chest.

Serrion stepped back, releasing his grip on his enemy. The still form of Jacques Andresen remained upright for a few moments against the wall. Serrion thought it was strange the way that the young man's back was arched out, away from the stone and tapestry.

As Serrion slowly realised what had happened, Jacques Andresen's body began to tumble forwards. There was a faint, sickening sucking sound and then he fell face down on the floor. Embedded in the wall behind him where it had been hurled by the explosion was one of the long dark splinters of the black staff of Atros.

Orianna and Serrion staggered from the great hall. Already the clouds of ravens, gulls and hawks were beginning to wheel away into the higher air above. Their angry cries and calls were now softened into normal birdsong, the commanding, controlling voice of their evil mistress now stilled and silent forever.

The rish too were on the run. It seemed as if all the spirit to fight had left them in the minutes between Piotre's disappearance and Jacques' death. Many had merely dropped their weapons and begun to flee as soon as the windows of the great hall had shattered. The pulver and Tarawen's rebels were already rounding up the final groups who still remained in the piazza. Serrion and Orianna watched one of them as he was chained up by Tarawen, who had a harsh smile spreading across his face.

The brother and sister looked up, craning their necks to see as the last of the birds disappeared into the grey clouds that were forming from the east. The same wind that brought the clouds hit their faces with a sudden cold gust and they shivered.

'Come on,' said Serrion. 'There are people that we need to see.' He gestured towards the anxious groups that were beginning to appear in a number of doorways. Some were already rushing across the piazza, chattering excitedly, congratulating the pulver and pointing towards the skies. They gathered in a small crowd at the bottom of the steps of the great hall.

Orianna and Serrion clung together, supporting each other. A cheer rose up to greet them, growing louder and louder as they descended.

Epilogue

When Helen stepped out of the pathway from Earth she did not attract any attention. No one in the happy crowds even noticed the flash of light behind them as she arrived.

She stood at the edge of the crowd. Serrion had not seen her yet. He was still being congratulated and helped through the crowds alongside Orianna. The cheering had reached a deafening level as word spread that the evil had been defeated! Jacques Andresen and Larena the Birdwoman were dead, and the black staff of Atros had been destroyed!

Serrion and Orianna did not smile however. Their faces were set in grim lines, each remembering what they had lost.

'I cannot tell him about Cleve Harrow yet,' Helen thought to herself. 'He is not ready. He could not cope with news of another betrayal, not yet, not now. Let him have this moment of victory.'

She turned and walked away from the cheering throng. She just wanted to go home now, to be with her mum and dad. This battle with Atros was over at last, but her head was still spinning with thoughts of the news that she would have to tell Serrion sooner or later, and those other troubles, much closer to home, that she knew it would lead to...

The end of 'The Beltheron Select'.
The adventures of Serrion, Helen and Orianna
conclude in 'The Beltheron Darkness' which will be
published in 2011.